Messenger

FULFILLMENT

PART II

MICHAEL POLOWETZKY

ISBN: 978-1-63950-094-9 (sc)
ISBN: 978-1-63950-095-6 (e)

Because of the dynamic nature of the Internet, any web addresses or links contained in this book may have changed since publication and may no longer be valid. The views expressed in this work are solely those of the author and do not necessarily reflect the views of the publisher, and the publisher hereby disclaims any responsibility for them.

Writers Apex

Gateway Towards Success

8063 MADISON AVE #1252
Indianapolis, IN 46227
+13176596889
www.writersapex.com

To: A

CONTENTS

MAGNIFICAT

*M*arie-Raymonde-Adrienne-Julienne-Michele de Valois, Duchesse Charpentier-Martignac is called *Raymonde* for short. Or, by her intimates: *Rose*. Never defeated, she is in addition, history's greatest female long distance runner, arguably the best female athlete of any kind. During the Lisbon Olympics, she established new time-records in winning for France the gold medal at Women's 5000 Meters and Women's 10,000 Meters. Uncontested victor too in the intervening Chicago World championships, she next took part in the Frankfurt Olympics. Here, she not only again won the gold medal at Women's 5000 Meters and Women's 10,000 Meters but also broke her own previously-set time records. That originally concluded her fleet-footed schedule. Raymonde/Rose never trained for or intended entering tracks' oldest, longest and most prestigious event.

"But then" explained the dainty champion to a swarm of newspaper journalists, photographers and television cameras after the deed was done, skimpy running suit now wrapped in *Tricoleur,* her pretty head crowned with fragrant laurels: "I heard the Still, Small Voice. And the Still, Small Voice whispered: 'Rose, Rose, the Marathon, the Marathon! Don't forget the Marathon!' At once I understood. I answered: *'My soul doth magnify the Lord and my spirit rejoices in God my savior. For He hath regarded the lowliest of His handmaidens. For behold, from henceforth all generations will call me blessed. For He that is mighty magnifies me and*

1

blessed is His name. His mercy is on them that fear Him throughout all generations '"

So, this singular girl besides again winning the Olympic gold medal at Women's 5000 Meters and Women's 10,000 Meters, also captured the gold medal at Women's Marathon. All three were accomplished in less than a week!

Mortal flesh, even the best skilled, can strain itself to just a finite degree. Eventually, the forever-unequaled record how—fast; far; high; long; well—any event in sports can be performed is reached. These ultimate records at Women's 5000 Meters, Women's 10,000 Meters, and Women's Marathon already belong to Raymonde.

On her triumphal return to Paris, "The Napoleon of Track" was invested into the *Légion d'Honneur*. "For," said part of the government's declaration printed in all newspapers, announced on all television, radio channels: "bringing the Republic of France matchless, undying achievement, demonstrating her nation's cultural spirit at its finest. She is the embodiment of all which is noblest in French womanhood."

Schools, hospitals, bridges, stadiums, plazas, avenues, parks, airports, highways, cars, sports clubs, woman's organizations, tunnels, canals, mountains, lakes, constellations, comets, space missions, to say nothing of: babies, dolls and pets were and still *are* frequently named after this nimble-footed girl. Her winning smile; gold medal-legs; high intelligence; melodic voice and refined, aristocratic personality all further contribute to her appeal among both the French public and sports enthusiasts across the world. Raymonde's fetching image is often seen on postage stamps, covers of magazines, on sweatshirts. Her hairdos are all-the-rage. She makes a fortune from her personal brand of running-shoes, the cameo-roles she performs in television shows and movies, through being photographed in perfume advertisements and by accepting invitations from prestigious couturiers to wear their latest gowns at various social functions.

After in Frankfurt setting the ultimate Olympic time records in her track events, Raymonde proceeded to Tokyo where she established the supreme time records for her events at World Championship games. For four successive years, she won the Boston and New York marathons, coming first across the finish line too in marathons held at Cape Town, Beijing, Paris, Madrid, Leningrad, Copenhagen, London, Sydney, Buenos Aires, Seoul and Los Angeles. The unmatchable time records for *in-door* Woman's 5000 Meters, Woman's 10,000 Meters and Woman's Marathon are hers as well. Raymonde is even the only non-US athlete featured on a *Wheaties* cereal box.

Soon bodyguards were required. First, to fend off the mob of hysterical international admirers and paparazzi chasing Raymonde everywhere she went; later, for protection against Muslim fanatics trying to assassinate her when running in Beirut and Algiers. She received an avalanche of marriage proposals. Continuing to triumph in every long distance race (inside *and* outside) she competed in over the next four years, the grand lady was universally expected repeating her brilliant triple victory at Frankfurt in the Singapore Olympics. Tragically, during an early 5000 Meter trial heat, Raymonde stumbled, damaging the cartilage of right leg and could not race again. With her sudden, unforeseen departure from the arena, sports lost a phenomenon never to be equaled or even approached.

How was Raymonde affected by her historic sports career cut-short? Already ensconced in the mind of countless millions across the planet—for males: as cult figure, secular icon, fantasy date, sex object; for women: offering them an assertive, independent and successful role model, her personal character and life story as appealing to *Feminists* as to social conservatives—she winning hearts both religious and agnostic, the international heroine experienced none of the fading-public attention Véronique suffered in classical ballet. As to how the injury affected her emotionally, Raymonde is a private individual. Perhaps that's only to be expected of long distance runners, most of whose waking hours are devoted to solitary racing around tracks or traversing alone cross-country. The Duchess also isn't just an Olympian. She is: a *lady*. And ladies don't—whine; use uncultivated language; belabor others with own private concerns; or otherwise make of themselves "an unseemly, unfeminine spectacle." The tremendous spiritual and mental-anguish the Duchess experiences daily because of losing her track career at its apex she confides to just one person.

Her Grace's ambitions however, aren't confined to track. They are dedicated above all to the Still, Small Voice. She wishes to give her faith living Witness employing the same commitment, enthusiasm used earlier to capture five historic Olympic gold medals. Annually, a notable percentage of the large, expertly-invested profits the Duchess obtains from sale of her own—popular brand of running-shoes, much-coveted fragrance, stylish cosmetics and chic intimate toiletries go to financing a private charity. This, dedicated to advancing the civil rights, education and careers of gifted but impoverished teenage girls from the Third World. If admittedly not as big as older, better known NGOs, *Raymonde's Girls* is far more effective than they in the results sought with more limited resources through its far superior management and aid targeting. As a private charity, too, *Raymonde's Girls* along with immigrant community counterpart *Raymonde's Girls (France)* doesn't need spending major parts of its annual budget courting politicians, maintaining a top-heavy bureaucracy, leading fund-raising campaigns and making television advertisements. Two years ago, the Duchess was selected by the *United Nations* to serve as international spokesman and goodwill ambassador for *UNICEF.*

Not without reason did Véronique Castellane, fearful her "Divine Child" was stalled in artistic creativity because of *Scatterbrained Female-*interference, seek-out her gold medalist-friend's assistance.

I

Like countless millions of Raymonde's other worshipful, devoted fans, Pascale was familiar with nearly every aspect of the Charpentier Saga. As the taxi carried her from *La Nouvelle Heloise* to this morning's encounter, Pascale noticed the vehicle navigating **Boulevard de Charpentier,** entering **Place de Charpentier,** crossing one bank of the Seine to other atop **Pont de Charpentier.** From first time seeing "Duchess Raymonde's exploits" on television, *Chere Petite* collected God-only-knows-how-many: photos; videos; coffee mugs; posters; playing-cards; tee-shirts; statuettes; flags; tennis caps and other pieces of paraphernalia each celebrating the triumphs of her heroine. That the two ladies might one day actually come face-to-face never dared enter this teenager's even wildest hopes.

"Still, the strangest things do happen!" Pascale observed silently upon being ushered to the great athlete's presence in an elegant first floor salon of sumptuous neoclassical palace surrounded by well-kept *Continental* gardens and high enclosing wall. "Still, the strangest things do happen."

The young guest was indescribably nervous. "I hope I make a good impression. I hope I make at least a half-decent impression!"

A week had passed since Pascale first called Véronique—*Mama*.

"Firebid provides you with excellent, splendid recommendations, Emmanuelle, Sweetheart" commented the Olympian. Like her prima ballerina-friend, Raymonde was in her elegant, genteel, highly-attractive, early-thirties. Thick, sinuous, coffee-and-cream color hair fell below her graceful bare shoulders. She wore impressive but unpretentious jewelry. Five-feet-nine-inches, tall for a woman, her lovely, unblemished skin and aristocratic face were applied just the proper touch of expensive fragrance and makeup, no more. An awe-inspiring personality seeming just stepped from a Gordon Parks photograph in *Vogue*, La Duchesse is one of those rare, magical, figures we all yearn for the privilege to simply, obey.

"Thanks so much Your Grace" replied her mesmerized-guest. She, making an instinctive deep curtsey and no less reverent-dip of head. "I hope I live up to it, Mistress. I hope you won't think Mme. Castellane was exaggerating!" Anxious cadence to words, limbs stiffening, girl cautiously adjusted the hem of her navy blue jacket.

"*Please!*" insisted the Grand Lady, motioning to a cherry wood red damask armchair beside blue, own.

Pascale smiled humbly.

Promptly seated in designated spot studiously upright, her pretty bare legs crossed, hands folded in lap, her eyes inspected carefully-selected clothes for possible oversights.

"You look lovely, Emmanuelle dear!" congratulated La Buchesse, reaching out to straighten her young guest's white bobbysocks. "Her

Grace is sure on visits you're always in your very best. Her Grace especially likes that skirt. It must be ever-so exciting to wear."

"Thank-you, Mistress. It certainly is!"

"You must tell where you found that skirt so Mistress can wear one too! When important ladies give compliments she'll tell them it was her little protégée's brilliant suggestion! Duchess Charpentier isn't one of those jealous females who doesn't admit receiving help from others."

"I will indeed tell, Mistress!"

"Mistress knows you will."

Two set of gray-green eyes linked long, deep, understanding.

Older of pair bestowed younger a soft, protective, blessing.

Breathing easier, her limbs relaxing, Pascale sat back in the richly upholstered-armchair.

"Would you enjoy tea, Emmanuelle, dear?" questioned Raymonde. "Mistress remembers vividly being your age. She lived in a convent in Normandy. With its renowned teaching Order, long dedication to female intellectual achievement, vast historic library, famous winding tunnels filled with historic letters and documents, all the daughters in our family have been educated in this convent since the Middle Ages. Several daughters in the Valois family also became the abbess! One of the current nuns came from England—Sister Madeleine Beauchamp. Sister Madeleine was—*still is*—a most sweet and encouraging lady. She was—*still is*—a superb instructor."

"Sister Madeleine is also the person inspiring me to race!" enlightened her adoring-Sidekick. "Sister Madeleine was the first saying I might make a name for myself on the track. At the beginning, Sister Madeleine was my coach and personal trainer. One doesn't think of nuns shouting—'Maintain a killer instinct, Rose;' 'Show absolutely no mercy, Rose!' 'Wish only to annihilate competition!" "Crush anyone with the audacity daring to oppose you!' So she did though, bless Sister Madeleine with her soft, pious, loving soul. 'A stadium' Sister Madeleine was fond of telling me, 'isn't a church, Rose! Humility gets you nowhere in sports! Show me a good loser and I'll show you a loser! The meek will *not* inherit the *finish line!*' When Mistress won her first gold medal she dedicated it to Sister Madeleine as was only just and proper and well deserved. But we can continue this subject another day."

"Besides my inspiration, my leader on the track" Raymonde added, fondly, "Sister Madeleine could—*still can*—be an excellent parent. Many of her little charges both past and present look upon Sister Madeleine as their true *Mama*! She taught us not only her country's language but also introduced us to her country's famous beverage. Once sampled, tea can hardly be done without! Mistress will be be delighted ordering some brought for you?"

"No, no, don't over-exert yourself Mistress!" begged Pascale, waving hands for emphasis, her immense jet-black hair obscuring face. "After all your famous races and after your terrible injury you must easily get tired! I'm fine and don't want exhausting you. I'd never want to make any trouble." The anxious girl received another incomparably warm, affectionate adult beam.

"Marcelle, *treasure*" the five-gold medal-chatelaine said to a Burmese girl Pascale's same age and physical dimensions, standing nearby. Like Pascale, the girl's white bobbysocks drooped to ankles as she listened enraptured by *Raymonde the Great's* every word. "Please be so kind as to bring the refreshments."

"Yes, Mistress!" chirped Marcelle. "Yes, Mistress, I'll bring refreshments!"

Excitedly, the energetic diminutive creature sped off, eager to demonstrate her sole desire in life was to faithfully serve an employer for whom she possessed boundless love and admiration.

"Don't run-too-fast, Sweetheart! Marcelle shouldn't tire her devoted, yearning, miniature self. Duchess Charpentier doesn't want her *Hummingbird* injured. She well understands her Marcelle is always the Duchess's eager, loyal, faithful, ever-dependable, helper."

Pascale observed atop adjoining ebony table a framed, color, studio-photograph of twin oriental girls aged five or six. "Are they yours, Mistress? Are you their Mama?"

"So they are, Dear! Thank-you for noticing. Yes, I'm their Mama—*adopted-Mama*. I found the twins in Laos during my first official trip as ambassador for *UNICEF*. The precious little darlings were almost naked and starving in that wretched idol-worshiping hamlet. I knew immediately I must own the adorable pair. So I arranged it. I brought the girls back with me to France, had them baptized, given Christian names and provided citizenship. I taught them to speak French, to know the *Catechism* and to recite with me daily the *Rosary*. There's no worry again of the dears starving, almost naked in some pagan forest. I'm not sending them for education at the convent in Normandy yet, however. The children possessed no proper family in Laos. Before school, they require some *personal, hugged, placed-on-lap care.*"

Raymonde warmly kissed Pascale on her lips.

She fondly stroked her eager new protégée's multitudinous jet black hair.

"That's the reason you were summoned today, Emmanuelle. Duchess Charepentier promised her daughters she'd obtain them an affectionate, protective, loyal *Big Sister*. An affectionate, protective, loyal *Big Sister* who desires nothing more in life than taking-care of her two little sisters—desires nothing else than playing-games with them both night and day—wants only to offer wise *Big Sister* encouragement, wise big sister-advice. Mama told her daughters the big sister she obtained for them has a background not entirely unlike theirs. The children are so excited to meet you, Emmanuelle!"

Pascale shifted in armchair for a better look, moving carefully so as not to hurt the upholstery.

She adjusted her skirt, crossed her bare legs opposite.

"What are their names, Mistress?"

"That one on the *left* is—Marie—named for Mistress's cousin, the abbess of St. Elisabeth's Benedictine convent. Such a sweet lady the abbess is, She writes me weekly. She was so ever-so kind when my parents died. Even though she's a cloistered nun and we've never actually met, I feel as if Mother Marie is always at my side eager to comfort me."

"How lovely."

"Thank, you, Dear"

"The other girl is—Albertine—named for her auntie, Mistress's younger sister."

"Didn't your younger sister also win a gold medal and set a record at the Olympics, Mistress?"

"So glad you remember, *Bunny Rabbit.* So she did! It was at Frankfurt. All the press attention was directed at me but no one should ever overlook Missy's splendid accomplishment. H pole vault. Her record is absolutely unchallenged to this very day!"

Pascale adjusted her socks.

Crossed pretty legs opposite.

Hem of short skirt receding.

"Of course" Raymonde stressed, "Missy and I were simply being good, dutiful children, obeying what we were instructed. We just wanted to show proper respect for our elders. My own adopted-daughter Marie wants to take-up Olympic archery or javelin when she's older. I said—'Mama will be delighted just as long as darling makes sure looking-out where she shoots her arrows, casts her javelins.' Albertine informs me her own ambition is an Olympic gold medal at long jump or high jump. Mama said—that's wonderful Dear, so long as Cherie doesn't break her little leg.'"

"Daughters in this family are sports enthusiasts," commented proud parent, beaming with rightful maternal pride. "There's none of that *Weaker Sex, Fragile Female* nonsense among the Charpentier ladies."

"Now observe *this*, Sweetheart." Chatelaine directed her guest's attention to a walnut, polished, antique, dark brown lowboy chest with polished brass drawer handles. Atop, was a framed photograph of Mme. de Charpentier's younger sister demonstrating celebrated prowess at her chosen field event.

"Sadly, goodhearted Missy was distracted from pole vaulting after the Frankfurt Olympics" Raymonde confided in mournful voice, her attractive face expressing immense intellectual and spiritual pain. It was a mental anguish combined with sense of personal guilt. One, as hard to bear as any blow inflicted physically. "All that innocent-idealism, sincere-altruism Missy possessed left her vulnerable to being taken advantage of. For as long as I can recall, Missy felt ashamed of being born into the aristocracy. She wished to atone for what she perceived as her deep sinfulness. She's far more devout Catholic than me. In another time and place, Missy would like my cousin, be a famous, much-respected, deeply-venerated abbess. Theologians from throughout Christendom would eagerly, regularly, turn to her for words of wisdom. Unfortunately for poor Missy, this is not another time and place."

"Following Missy's historic victory in the Frankfurt Olympics" continued Raymonde, "she was approached by members of the West German urban guerrilla network *The Red Brigades.* 'We're struggling to bring equality to the working class, to overthrow the oppression of international capitalism' Missy was told. 'If someone as distinguished as you both in athletics and in the ancient French nobility joins our ranks, Countess Martignac, it'll be a tremendous boost to the cause.' So, the good-hearted, well-meaning child who in another time and place would now be a famous, much-respected, deeply-venerated abbess whom theologians from all over Christendom eagerly, regularly, sought-out for her words of wisdom, instead, joined the *Red Brigades.*"

Raymonde paused.

"After years as a fugitive, years as a notorious anti-*NATO* and anti-*EU* radical, Missy wanted across the Continent 'dead or alive,' Missy was finally caught attempting to blow up the largest armaments factory in Europe. She betrayed, as so often happens, by one of her own! At the trial, Missy was insistent she long ago dedicated her entire life, body and soul, 'to liberating the slaves of capitalism.' She was sentenced to life imprisonment. Today, the few still recalling her name think of Missy only as a *Cold War* era, internationally-hunted terrorist. They don't remember she was also a sweet, idealistic, well-meaning spirit and magnificent athlete."

Raymonde broke off to wipe teary eyes with silk handkerchief.

"Such a waste of a precious, noble soul" she lamented. "It was entirely my own fault. As her elder, more adult sibling, I should've been far stricter in who I permitted Missy coming in contact. God be praised Mama was no longer alive to learn what my negligence permitted to happen!"

Raymonde earnestly crossed herself, kissed the silver crucifix on necklace.

"Well, God has a purpose for it–or, so at least Mother Marie and Sister Madeleine say I'm supposed to believe. I make it a sacred point visiting Missy each summer so she can receive and enjoy some good, affectionate chatter. I made it a solemn personal obligation to visit Missy each summer so she can receive some warm hugs and kisses, some nice long *Girl Talk,* so Missy can hear some words of love, sympathy and encouragement. I want Missy to always know there are people in the world who still cherish her precious noble-hearted soul. I always send her presents on her birthday and on Christmas. To the extent she and I are permitted, we correspond too. It's my absolute duty since it was my negligence which let Missy get into this problem in the first place."

"My daughters ask repeatedly" explained adoptive-mother, "*Mama, where did Auntie Missy go?' 'Mama, why can't Auntie Missy visit us anymore? We'd so much like to see Auntie Missy again?' 'Did we hurt Auntie Missy's feelings? 'We so love our Auntie Missy!'* I think soon I'll need telling them the truth."

Such enigmatic words instantly captured Pascale's deep interest. She'd much like to elaboration but sensed querying further on the subject was inappropriate. Instead, she returned her attention to the picture of the twins. Unlike most, this duo weren't dressed alike. One child wore a red dress, the other azure. If each had white socks, one wore black patent leather shoes, the other red mary-janes.

"Yes, I've clothed them differently" enlightened their adoptive-mother. "Having them go around alike would be cute but I wish making sure each girl realizes she's an individual. I don't want them suffering psychological problems caused by being apart."

"So lovely your twin daughters are, Mistress!" complimented Pascale. "Such pretty names too!" Resting her on bare knees, supporting chin with palms, Pascale inspected the photograph long and closely. Searching, to discover the personality of each child, she also hoped to locate by chance her own spiritual connection.

Where was it to be found?

Curve of ear, angle of nose, height of eyes perhaps?

Maybe: depth of mouth or contour of jaw?

As girl was wrapped in contemplation, hostess gently stroked guest's jet-black mane descended to shins.

"Many excellent things have been reported about you, Emmanuelle" reiterated Raymonde after time, glancing momentarily at sentences written on yellow notepad. "Firebird praise syour *loyalty, piety* and *earnestness.*"

Guest smiled deferential while discreetly hitching her panties.

"Firebird also praises your *inquisitiveness* and *creativity*"

"I hope it may be so, Mistress."

Refreshments arrived.

"Here they are Your Grace!" announced Marcelle, breathless, she just scurried-back carrying a sterling silver tray with elegant antique tea service and bowl of fresh fruit atop. She placed the tray down carefully atop a fine oak table with marble surface, then curtseyed deeply. "Here they are, Your Grace!"

"Thank-you so much Marcelle, darling."

"Will there be anything else you need me for Your Grace? I'm ready! I'm ever-so ready to serve! Your Grace's slightest wish is my command!"

"Then go back at once to your room my faithful Marcelle and complete the newest book-report Duchess assigned. You're clearly developing a brilliant, exquisite in-born gift for words. You're starting to display a unique, beautiful, natural talent for expressing thoughts with ink-on-paper. Duchess knows her polymath-*Hummingbird* is blessed by God with an excellent ability to provide Christendom many lofty, unforgettable historic insights. Insights on subjects most of our witless sex never just once consider. No *Scatterbrained Female*, you Marcelle! You're going to be famous one day—a renowned petite theologian, an honored junior-academician!"

"I'll go at once Duchess!" piped Marcelle, bubbling with happiness. "I'll go back to my room and complete the newest book-report assigned me! Thank-you so-so-so much for your confidence and trust in me, Duchess!"

"Duchess, promises to one day get Marcelle's book-reports, Marcelle's book reviews, published. Now, off!"

Marcelle scurried-away.

"The first three attributes listed in Firebird's recommendation are satisfactory enough" commented Raymonde when she and Pascale gain alone. "That Mistress expects *loyalty, piety* and *earnestness* exhibited by her household at all times, goes-without-saying. However, the latter two attributes are what caught Mistress's special, eager attention. It's for these she invited you for a *chat* this morning Mi! Listen just now— *chat*! Those years with England's Sister Madeleine left me with more than a fondness for running and a liking for tea! Still sure you don't want any? There're nearly one thousand different kinds of tea, Sister Madeleine explained. They come from: China; India; Pakistan; Ceylon; Bangladesh; Persia—such a nicer, more romantic name than *Iran*."

"Yes, it is, Mistress! It's so ancient, so beautiful—and now so far away!"

"Tea also comes from Thailand and from Burma where precious Marcelle was born. Also from France's former colonies in Indochina— even Russia? Liking tea enables you to learn a lot about geography, discover many things about exotic lands and interesting peoples far beyond the seas. Want a cup?"

"No, no, Mistress!"

"What about a piece of fruit?"

"Please don't worry yourself, Mistress."

"Mme. de Charpentier is in the mood. Would her *Pet* object?"

"Of, course not, Mistress!"

The bowl of fresh, firm, colorful juicy citrus was as lovely as the one depicted in the Cézanne painting visible on the left wall. The Grand Lady selected a pear, provided her shy companion an encouraging wink, then took a genteel, bite. She winked encouragingly, again. Her facial gesture indicated satisfaction. Even the movements of the Duchess's jaws, thought, Pascale, were, so elegant, matchless, refined!

"Tasty! Are you absolutely sure you don't want something, *Pet*? There are also, let's see, there are: grapes, oranges, apples, tangerines and plumbs. Mme. de Charpentier wouldn't want her Emmanuelle going-hungry. What would Sister Madeleine say? 'A growing, girl needs nourishment, requires *Vitamin-C!*'"

Pascale reluctantly spied a plumb.

13

So: fresh; large; firm; smooth; deep-colored.

So: much better than any ever to be found in a store.

Her right hand approached it furtive.

Soon, fast, guiltily withdrew.

Grand Lady signaled her to try again.

For second time, a cautious, deliberate advance ensued.

Adult smile beckoning child, continue exploratory expedition.

Slowly, slowly, bit by bit, youthful fingers proceeded.

Adult's warm, gray-green eyes urged hesitant treasure-seeker on.

Gradually, gradually, little by little

Until at last, unimagined goal reached.

Girl's hand speedily retreating with succulent quarry lest privilege, be revoked.

Elder's gentle diamond-gaze twinkling approval

"'Rose, you should learn more about this exceptional little Darling!'" the Duchess recounted after a moment. "'All the—*loyalty, piety, earnestness*—in the world won't make up for lack of *inquisitiveness,* for absence of an independent and searching mind! Sincerity and a good heart alone can't fix a thorny problem or offer a new and better idea! As for unquestioning—*loyalty,* it's not worth much compared with freely-given loyalty and needed, timely—*creativity*!' Mistress doesn't want a toady, a foot-licker girl who simply parrots her *Better's* every word!

Hostess motioned Guest take a second plumb.

This time Guest felt no inhibition.

Expression on adolescent painted lips registering delight

Don't they taste *so* good, *Pet*?"

"Yes indeed, Mistress!"

Ladies gestured agreement.

Each crossed own pretty legs opposite, same.

"It's time for tea. Mistress knows her *Bluebird* will enjoy."

"Thank-you most kindly, Mistress. I'll be delighted!"

Raymonde presented a lace napkin. "Don't get a stain on that nice blouse, *Bunny Rabbit*. Spots are so difficult removing. Surely you devoted much time selecting this one for your visit."

"Yes, Mistress, spots are! I'll be careful. I promise!"

Grand Lady acknowledged warmly.

"Mistress knows you will, darling! That's another reason Sweetheart was invited here this morning."

Sewn by skillful little feminine hands long ago in Normandy convent, the napkin was no less beautiful than the fingers currently providing it. Charming antique tea cup and saucer harked to stirring times as well.

"This tea service comes from before the *Revolution*," informed the Grand Lady. "It's called *Sevres*. Made entirely by hand and to order! Difficult to imagine how the Hoi-polloi and unwashed-cutthroats didn't get their grubby paws on it! Remember what Talleyrand said? 'He who has not lived before the *Revolution* will ever understand how sweet life can be!' Let's hope, these pieces provide we ladies at least a little indication!"

"I've seen these tea services in museums, Mistress?" remarked Pascale, both impressed and disconcerted. "Are you sure I ought to drink from them?"

"Mistress knows *Angel* possesses all the proper *Old World* feminine grace. She knows her *Angel* is unquestionably a little lady!"

Hostess poured her guest a cup of tea.

Guest brought the cup to her lips.

"Mmmmm! That tastes so-so-good, Mistress!"

"Mme. de Charpentier knew her *Robin Redbreast* would enjoy a cup! This variety of brew is called *Russian Caravan Tea*. There's something—enticingly Asiatic, something—irresistibly *girl-thrown-over-a-saddle-and-galloped-off-with*—about the taste! It reminds one of sultans, courtesans, mysterious journeys, flying carpets, grand viziers, secret passageways, and lusting harems. Don't you think so, too?"

Guest indicated in affirmative, crossing legs opposite.

"And camels, too, Mistress!"

"Better keep on-your-guard with those nasty beasts! Tommy says they bite."

"Ouch!"

"Not that Mistress was unlucky enough experiencing it herself. She's simply going by what Tommy, pardon, *President Belanger*, recounted about his recent summit meeting. Tommy said being bitten by a camel was terribly unpleasant. The nasty, ugly beast seemed happy about it, Tommy insisted."

"Ooh!"

"Of, course, Emmanuelle mustn't believe everything she's told!"

"That's so correct, Mistress!"

The ladies gestured dainty agreement.

"You've too been in my part of the world, Mistress?" inquired Pascale, jet-black mane again over face. The huge red satin bow atop hair grown as signature to her as Churchill's cigar, was fast unraveling.

"Yes, indeed *Bunny Rabbit*" answered the Grand Lady, affectionately. "Mistress traveled there a number of times. You may see some photograph albums upstairs if you're really interested. Although there've been no visits recently, of course."

As if her legal possession and spiritual guardianship officially transferred from one benefactress to next, the latter, instead of refastening loose bow on girl's mane, removed it, altogether.

Two pair of gray-green feminine eyes linked long, deep, understanding.

Pascale felt another's tender, guardian's love touch her heart.

A larger, wiser being's warm, comforting, un-felt embrace.

"Travel is fun and mind-expanding," continued Grand Lady. "Mistress purchased Marcelle while on one of her journeys as *UNICEF* ambassador."

"**PURCHASED?**" cried Pascale, recoiling with alarm. She, instantly remembering her first encounter with Mme. Castellane and how Véronique pledged always protecting the homeless Middle Eastern waif "from those scoundrels already out-on-the-prowl for simple, naïve, goodhearted little things like you." Sinister images from literature, sculpture, current events and cinema raced vividly through adolescent mind. "**PURCHASED?**"

"That's precisely how my cousin the abbess of St. Elisabeth's reacted!" giggled Raymonde, she giving Pascale a peck on lips. "'What kind of perverse, criminal, diabolical scheme are you suddenly up-to, Rose?' Mother Marie wrote. 'Have you now become a procurer, become a merchant in *White Slavery*?' Sister Madeleine also dispatched me a similarly disparaging letter. 'Shame on you, Rose! Shame on you!' Sister Madeleine scolded me. 'Where were you taught to engage in this monstrous, foul, unchristian business! Certainly not here at the convent! How could this evil trait arise in a once so pious little girl?' Both Mother Marie and Sister Madeleine normally possess the most superb, delicate, ladylike penmanship. This time however their messages were written in the most frantic, near-indecipherable scribble! My cousin and former track coach also summoned me back to their convents to give me a severe talking-to! The Secretary General of the United Nations even needed to call a televised-press conference in order to explain what actually happened."

"It was indeed at first a purely sordid commercial transaction, *Bunny Rabbit*" the satisfied customer elaborated. "Mistress knows it sounds positively—Delacroix-painting, Roman orgy, Muslim Fundamentalist, Hollywood, American Confederacy, primitive, Vikings, Asiatic. However, there was no alternative. Mistress was accompanying her chum Tommy—*President Belanger*—to one of his interminable diplomatic summits. It wasn't held not in one of those pagan countries either! Parents were eagerly selling, yes *selling* their daughters! The parents, yes the *parents* approached and offered Mistress to *purchase* Marcelle! Can you believe it, Darling? They offered selling their-own-flesh-and-blood! And this wasn't in one of those countries where people run-around naked and beat on drums! These weren't the savages in those photographs from *National Geographic Magazine* boys so enjoy!"

"No, Mistress's *Robin Redbreast*!" stressed Raymonde. "This was a country in which the natives wear clothes! So what was I supposed to do? Refuse? Tell the scoundrels—'I'll let your daughter suffer because I oppose child trafficking? Let poor little Marcelle be sent to a brothel so I can feel all-high-minded-and-virtuous?' Talk about hypocrisy! Talk about taking the Lord's name in vain, bearing false witness! I'd be like the Levite in the story of the *Good Samaritan?* You know the story don't you?"

"Yes, Mistress"

"But of course. Firebird tells me you daily read the Bible and recite the *Rosary*. As Christ tells us in that parable we must demonstrate our faith and devotion through action not just idle words. So, Mistress *purchased* Marcelle returned with her to France."

"Travel is fun, mind-expanding" added the five-time Olympic gold medalist, her melodic voice again, queenly. 'Unlike poor Marcelle, Mistress luckily never needed to *purchase* Emmanuelle from *White Slavery*. For all the world knows, today might not at all be the first time you and Mme. de Charpentier have met. Our families might have once been old friends!"

"So nice if it was so, Mistress!"

"In any event, Emmanuelle, this is our first opportunity being alone together for a true *Woman-to-Woman* conference, first chance for some real good *Girl Talk*. There are none of those bothersome, full-of-themselves characters with trousers present to monopolize our conversation!—None, of those stupid, vain characters with trousers instantly feeling upset whenever they not constant center of ladies' attention—forever needing ladies to bolster their own fragile, little boy-egos—never permitting ladies to make their own decisions!"

"I pray it is so, Mistress!" reiterated Pascale. "We can have a true *Woman-to-Woman conference*. We can have some real good *Girl Talk*. And do so, without anybody with trousers bossing-us-around!"

She pondered.

Had Pascale already met Mme. de Charpentier? Not simply in Paris at the Place de Vosges or along the embankment but earlier still, back in the Middle East? Father enjoyed inviting distinguished westerners to the Kedari family compound. Several, among them women, were French. All, were introduced to Father's 'ever-so *Accomplished'* daughter Chere Petite. Could she, therefore have known the great Olympian too in earlier, happier times? In the end, if clear recollection couldn't confirm fond hope, it also failed disprove.

In case evidence of the two's previous contact was available today in their current surroundings, Pascale's eager, investigative, adolescent, feminine gray-green eyes inspected the elegant *Louis XV Style* parlor. First, she surveyed the over-stuffed, damask furniture, next, the large

French Windows. She shifted attention to the chamber's mirrors, crystal chandelier, its Saffavid Dynasty Persian carpet. Her gaze at last came to rest on the private museum collection of family portraits hanging regally from all the four papered-walls.

"All of them are so snooty-looking" Pascale concluded. "They clearly think they're my *Betters."* Painted over succeeding centuries by Durer, Holbein, De la Tour, Poussin, Claude Lorain, Chardin, Vignée-Le Brun, David, Ingres, Géricault, Delacroix, Courbet, Manet, Renoir, Degas, Cezanne, Laurencin, Matisse, Modigliani—each earlier Duc and Duchesse de Charpentier looked so self-important, so-sure-of-themselves. They likely hadn't the slightest appreciation of receiving the chance to be recorded on canvas for posterity by famous artists. "Artists like me were in those lords and grand dames' eyes just uncouth lackeys they could idly kick in the backside!"

"Some of those arrogant characters" she further decided, "look so stupid in their silly wigs and tortuously-tight knee breeches, corsets, stays. Those imperious ladies—if they truly were—*ladies*—look ridiculous with two-foot-high hair, hoop skirts giving them no choice but entering rooms sideways! More than a few of those nasty bitches and those lords-of-the-manor who never left the poor scullery maids alone, certainly well-deserved going to the guillotine or having a bomb thrown in their lap! They received just what was coming to them!"

Could someone descended from these haughty characters be one of Pascale's own long-lost intimates? Not likely!

"Of course, everyone has unpleasant relatives," she reminded herself. "We all possess a few blackguards, harpies in our family backgrounds, even someone as saintly as Father. Still, we also aren't gingerbread men! Times, events, customs change the way later generations view the world and care about others."

"Life can be so surprising, Sweetheart" interjected Raymonde. "It's so full of ironies. Don't you agree, *Pet?* Some people we assume intimately associated, were in fact, not so at all? Did you know Elizabeth I and Mary, Queen of Scots never met? Neither, did Tolstoy and Dostoyevsky, Napoleon and Beethoven! Others, we assume far apart, were actually quite close. Did you know Clarence Darrow voted for William Jennings

Bryan all three times?" She returned decorated teapot to service tray, brought forward collection of fine pastries.

This time, Pascale eagerly took a yummy piece.

"Mmmmm! Mmmmm! Delicious, delicious, Mme. de Charpentier!"

"Madame wonders if she might be privileged benefiting from Emmanuelle's celebrated *helpfulness* from time-to-time?" queried Raymonde, crossing her pretty aristocratic legs in sheerest hose crossing opposite. "Madame thought she might on occasion rely on her *Robin Redbreast's invaluable* assistance. And to do so too even if it turns out, we ladies are actually only recent acquaintances? Perhaps, *Angel* might eventually regard me as her own intimate, trusted girlfriend—a girlfriend, always ready to change her course of action if someone younger, more *inquisitive—of*fers a better proposal?"

"You're much smarter than me, Mistress!" pledged junior-Rembrandt, sinuous jet-black mane obscuring her face. Quickly erect in armchair, she again employed small hands for emphasis. "You're much smarter than me! You know far more about the world than I ever will!"

Raymonde smiled back affectionate, protective..

She stroked her awestruck little companion's soft, unblemished cheeks.

"No, no Emmanuelle, you *Priceless Innocent*. Behind all this pomp-and-circumstance, I'm no one special. In fact, I'm really quite ordinary. Not noteworthy at all! You, by contrast, speak six foreign languages, can engrave, paint frescoes! I attend Mass at a different church than the one presided over by Father Richard. However, I've been to your church on occasion. I've seen what Firebird enjoys calling 'the New Arena Chapel.' It's brilliant! It's the work of a second Giotto if my own opinion is of any value. If the just three completed-frescoes are so magnificent, just imagine how grand and glorious will be those yet to come! If *Pet* at last gets back in the mood to paint more rescoes, Mistress will do all humanly possible to provide encouragement and advise. Why, Mistress will see to it there's a public exhibition with television coverage. It can easily and in little time be arranged."

"Stop talking in that—icky, gross, terrible, dreadful, awful, silly, stupid, foolish, mean, hateful, degrading, unfair, rotten, horrible, bad, nasty, wrong, not-right, way about yourself, please!" blurted-out Pascale impassioned, mop of jet-black hair in face. She, abruptly abandoning humble speech to address her teemed hostess as if a social equal. "Stop! You're the most-*special,* most-*remarkable* lady I've ever met! I think you're so-so extremely smart! I think you're so-so *Accomplished*! You're the most *Accomplished* lady I've ever seen! You're the most *Accomplished* lady in-the-entire-world! As for foreign languages, I've just a natural facility! Painting, engraving, drawing: it's the same!"

"That's so kind of you, Mademoiselle" answered La Duchesse, her refined, melodic voice as–magisterial, aloof, imperious, as just moment earlier–welcoming, loving, gentle. She, delivering a subtle but clear, mistakable message: '*Chere Petite* must never again address her regal benefactress in anything but a deferential manner.' Leaving Pascale in no doubt from start of the two's special relationship which partner made the decisions, which one led, which, followed.

"But don't be overly-modest Child," added La Duchesse. "Females today should learn to stop *that-kind-of-thing.* One can't become fluent in six foreign languages and develop innate artistic talent, as easily as pick-up good manners and taste for fashion!"

She crossed her legs opposite.

"If you say so" endorsed *Drooped Bobbysocks,* crossing own legs opposite, same.

"Mistress isn't one of those famous people hanging from the walls," confided Her Grace. "Mistress perceived early in life she wasn't 'clever.' She knew that behind all her celebrated track ability, sophistication, good looks, social refinement, expensive upbringing, she was actually no-one-in-particular. Remember: 'All that glisters is not gold.' Luckily, this unpleasant discovery provided unique insight into others.–Bit of recompense, don't you think, Child?"

Drooped Bobbysocks nodded obediently, smiled dutiful.

"Having mastered fakery so well" explained the Olympian, now in protective, maternal voice, "Mistress has no difficulty spotting it in others! She's no problem determining which rare female is actually intelligent and which, as usual, is just pretending! You, Child, are a genius! Gifted, talented more than your innocent soul is capable of even dreaming! Take Mistress's word for it! She might not possess brains herself, but she clearly knows, who, *does*!"

"If you say so"

"Yes, Mistress *says so*!"

Mme. de Charpentier glanced at delicate diamond wrist watch. "It's time you were introduced to the other children. Something else Mistress understands is—motherhood. She knows her twins will benefit tremendously from *Bunny Rabbit's* care!"

Near the upright framed photograph of the twins was another carefully preserved color image. It, taken at the Frankfurt Olympics. On the left in this second picture, stood track coach-Sister Madeleine, her lovely face and graceful body clothed in a long black habit and veil, white wimple. *Rosary* beads and chain with wooden crucifix tied at narrow waist, her sculpted arms queenly akimbo. Teary-eyed, the majestic nun glowed with all possible maternal satisfaction. At center of picture, Raymonde in skimpy running suit, five historic gold medals around slender neck, stood atop winner's podium. *Tricoleur* in left hand, her right delivered proud salute as French flag was raised and band played *La Marseillaise*. A sweet, virginal, hopeful, expression of delight was on champion's pretty teenage face. It was the exact same expression Pascale would strike were she in situation.

"Mistress?"

"Yes"

"Can I have your autograph?"

"Oh, but of course, *Pet*."

Raymonde took pad and fountain-pen from drawer in ebony table.

> ***To: my dearest friend, confidante and companion, Emmanuelle***
>
> ***From: her own dearest guardian, teacher and protector, Rose***

CHERISHED MEMORIES

....

*T*wo years passed.

Twenty-four months elapsed since Pascale became a member of the Charpentier household.

For both art and history these were heady-times.

Just as Véronique guaranteed, Pascale conquered her creative block.

The woman released from the unclean Spirits; Christ driving the moneychangers from the temple; Mary Magdalene; The Last Supper; Christ in the Garden of Gethsemane; Christ Betrayed; St. Veronica on the Road of Sorrow; The Crucifixion; The women discovering the empty tomb—these, and yet additional masterpieces, each: near Life-size, sixty-four in all, came to grace what Véronique (opinion unprejudiced by a Mama's natural inclination to favor own children) rightly describes as "my daughter's New Arena Chapel." Unfortunately, the day such great frescoes and their Little Giotto became recognized, appreciated outside the 5th and 16th Arrondissement of Paris, was still to dawn.

I

This picture isn't perfect of course" admitted Pascale upon completing her latest drawing. She sat leisurely one afternoon within a wide, enclosed, blooming garden. "But then, no attempt to wrest control of Nature is *perfect*. Full success always slips just beyond mere mortals' grasp. I've seen a number of famous—very—famous paintings in which

I've detected a little detail omitted or a small feature portrayed not quite as it should. An angle here ever-so slightly too severe; a curve *there* just-so faintly under-emphasized."

"And in the end" she observed in same philosophical mood, closing yellow-covered sketchbook and placing it back in khaki bag, "what does *perfect* mean? Compare, for instance nudes by Rubens and by Cezanne or, country scenes of Gainsborough and Monet; the world according to Cimabue and the world according to Pollock; Ice Age bison of the Lascaux Caves and buffaloes by Remington. A complex design, in other cases a single dot! Each, on first glance is so different, all, on closer inspection possess the same magical 'I don't know what'-quality. If all the creative minds of history can't agree on what exactly *perfect* means, who am little me to claim I know or can define the answer better!"

"Anyway" reflected the girl, pushing tresses of thick jet-black hair from pretty face, "if we actually knew the answer we'd then be left with no further worthwhile reason to even live! A world possessing no objective to reach, no problem to solve, no argument to settle, will be a terribly boring one! Life will be reduced to just one long tea-time conversation where all the ladies are expected to agree. Ick! No place for an artist! Beauty, is only born in times of struggle. Perhaps God wants it this way, too."

"Perhaps" concluded Pascale, crossing herself, "God selected artists— yes, that's, right—that's including even—me—to each individually deliver His world an important, a critical lesson?

"Mi!" suddenly observed a familiar voice, just behind. "*Robin Redbreast* appears so solemn, grave suddenly! You've got heady, thoughts to-tackle, hey? Weight of all, the, world placed upon your tender shoulders, no? Well, artists, philosophers are given to deep reflection. They reside on higher plain than petty mortals. What do Germans call it? Angst or is it *Sturm und Drang.*"

"Mistress!" exclaimed Pascale, turning around with embarrassment, her shin-length jet-black mane thrown all in disorder. Swiftly putting sketchbook and colors aside, so, arms might assist mouth, brow and eyes, she offered a fervent apology. "Were you here a long time, Mistress?"

Snap, snap, snap, snap, further ladylike camera snaps

"Only five minutes, Bunny Rabbit?" said Raymonde in harmonious, genteel cadence. She rewound the expensive Japanese gadget, re-aimed and took additional pictures. A soft breeze against the *Olympian's* short white dress provided better illustration to her long, firm, smooth legs in shimmering silk pantyhose. The loose, revealing garment added further emphasis to entire body's graceful contours visible just beneath. Her thick coffee-and-cream color hair under large white chapeau reached almost to waist. As, always, La Duchesse possessed a haunting, beckoning, vulnerable fragrance; one, seemingly all her own.

Snap, snap, snap, snap

"Five minutes?" repeated Pascale anxiously. "So terribly, rude, impolite, silly and wrong of me not noticing your presence, Mistress! When coming here with my colors and sketchbooks the rest of humanity for me soon fades away. I become absorbed in my own private little universe. For me, there's personally nothing more fine-looking and thought-provoking than a place, a figure, a view, an object, or just something-or-other I can draw. For everyone else I must appear a mad crackpot or someone awfully opinionated and full-of-herself. Ooh!"

"Not at all B*luebird*!" purred the Olympian, welcoming-resolve on face. "An artist-at-work is so-lovely to behold, so-precious. Rose frequently comes to look-on without you realizing." She raised the Japanese gadget to record again. "Just keep in that precious position for a few more seconds."

"Certainly"

"Let Rose see more of her Emmanuelle's splendid, thighs."

"Is this better, Mistress?" asked the girl pulling back the hem of her short skirt.

"Excellent! A really sexy *Little Thing* you are!"

Snap, snap, snap, camera snap, click, click.

"Ah! Out of film!" pretty, aristocratic newcomer lamented, stiffening red painted lips. "Rose knew she should've brought another roll. Still, Rose was able capturing some more good images of her *Pet*."

"Now hand me your latest sketchbook!" she then ordered imperiously. "No more foolishness!"

"Yes, of course Mistress, *here"* answered Pascale, obediently handing her sketchbook over for inspection.

"Excellent! Excellent! Fine work, Emmanuelle! Splendid! Superb!" cried Mme. de Charpentier, at last. She added emphasis to her appraisal by providing Little Giotto a warm peck on lips. "The rankest amateur can tell Love's got deep thoughts at present—can see you're expressing important concerns! There's something about the autumn which truly inspires you!"

One of Pascale's latest drawings especially grasped Mme. de Charpentier's attention. She placed the picture at arm's-length so discerning adult eyes might judge from objective distance. Soon bringing it close, she moments later returned the picture to a distance. "This particular picture" extolled the Grand Lady unconsciously shifting her conversational voice from traditional aloof *Vous* into intimate, comradely *Tu,* "captures my admiration, my respect, my—shock-and-awe. No, no! My reaction is—is suddenly so hard to express! Love's picture possesses a singular—I can't quite describe it'—quality' in it! The same magical, glorious unique—'I don't know what'—quality of truly priceless art!"

"So glad you enjoy this afternoon's work, Mistress!" meowed talented-protégée gratefully. "The sketch you're looking at now is also my own favorite. I drew it second to last. The chalk simply started moving. In the same manner authors claim characters take control of stories. 'Don't write about me this way, author! Write about me that way!' This is far from the first time I selected this subject. Instantly, I understood a similar chance wasn't going to come again—ever! Only now would the subject appear as it did. Only now could an artist record it in such a meaningful, perceptive way. So, a force within me led my hands to draw the picture as I did, Mistress!"

"Indeed, my own, my very own special Emmanuelle!" answered Raymonde. "Brilliant! Seize the Moment!"

She gazed again enraptured at the girl's tantalizing sketch.

"Your work certainly has a—message–*Bunny Rabbit*! And it's a major, significant, crucial message, too! As *Pet* mentioned, one need only glance at it for a moment to understand why this picture had to be drawn! The message, the message, the message! How shall I describe the, significance?—It's, it's, it's almost, frightening!—Odd, the way I'm suddenly at-a-loss-for-words, lacking in vocabulary! Frightening, frightening! No! No! Frightening isn't correct, no, no! The message isn't frightening. There's nothing dreadful, foreboding, terrifying or scary in what your creation tells us. It gives the world a brilliant message."

She paused.

"Yes, yes, Mistress?" pleaded Pascale. "Tell me what I want to inform the world?"

"Your announcement to the world" said Raymonde at last, eyes still riveted on the picture her little companion drew, "Your announcement to the world—is too important, profound for me, to fully comprehend all-at-once."

II

"Emmanuelle?" inquired young friend one gentle, fecund, spring morning.

"Yes, Mlle. Albertine" replied Pascale, voluminous tresses of jet-black by now fallen well down attractive legs. The huge, red, satin hair bow, once as emblematic as was to Churchill his cigar, Pascale eagerly dispensed with as soon as arriving in new home. Currently, she wore a white sleeveless blouse, a *Royal Stuart* tartan, white socks, black flat shoes fastened with buckle.

"Emmanuelle? I've got a question."

The two girls, physically identical except in color of mane, were seated atop the newly-mowed lawn of extensive, rambling *British Style* garden. The air was fresh, temperature just right, the delft color sky clear. Last night it rained heavily, at last disbursing the grim, thick, depressing, battleship-gray cloud-cover hiding the sun for over a week. A residue of the welcomed, long-awaited downpour was still detected by touching patches of moist earth, or watching the delicate, flirtatious shimmer created when sun beams met wet grass.

Also in the extensive, rambling, *British Style* garden were: clutches of wide, verdant chestnut and plain trees, scattered boulders covered with moss, *Augustan Age* marbles depicting beautiful nude feminine Greek deities abducted by lustful, handsome satyrs without the nymphs putting up much fight. At the shore of a fish-stocked, swan-cruising artificial lake was a neoclassical, Ionic-columned mausoleum. Atop a hill at the property's center, just left of where the girls now sat, abutted on three sides by terraced flowerbeds was Palais Charpentier, the family's impressive and architecturally-significant early-seventeenth century *Baroque* mansion.

The heavy, tall, iron, outer gate allowing just a select few entrance to the grounds is located at No. 4 Rue Marina Tsvetaeva in the 16th Arrondissement, beyond the Trocadero. If still found administratively within the western perimeter of the French capital, the extensive estate's four meter high, thick, ivy-covered redbrick enclosing walls easily give those on the grounds and in the mansion a firm impression of living in the countryside.

"Ouch!" muttered Albertine, grimacing. She supported promising outset-of-puberty feminine torso upright through placing both arms behind back, hands resting on a picnic blanket seen better days. Young athlete wore pink shorts, a white tee-shirt bearing *Frankfurt Games* logo, pair of Raymonde's prestigious brand of running shoes. One leg, child projected out, the other she held erect, folded at newly skinned knee. "Ouch!"

"Sorry it hurts, Mlle. Albertine" apologized Pascale in protective, maternal voice, she sitting cross-legged beside, applying ointment to younger companion's wound. "This ointment may sting but it's also by far the best medication."

In spite of her recent fall, it was plain to anyone watching the child's assiduous daily practice that Albertine too was a future champion. Like her adoptive-mother, adoptive-auntie and grandmother she also was certain one day bringing home for the non-*Weaker Sex*-Charpentier ladies yet another track-and-field Olympic gold medal. One, never to be equaled, let alone surpassed in the records of achievement at chosen events—hurdles, long jump. Currently, she was practicing the latter.

"What was your question, Mlle. Albertine?"

"Emmanuelle, are zebras black with white stripes or black with white stripes? It's long fascinated me. Sometimes I wonder about the answer so much at night I can't sleep." Aside from destined for sports fame, Albertine was undeniably summoned to a lifetime's noble calling. She was without doubt possessed of a *vocation*, that of—philosopher.

"Hmm" contemplated Pascale, finishing medical treatment. She closed her gray-green eyes. Inhaled deeply, savored long the sweet aroma of newly-mowed grass. "Hmm—I'd wager—black with white stripes. Of course, remember what I've taught?"

"Don't simply accept someone else's opinion as the truth!"

"Excellent! And don't ever forget it, Mlle. Albertine!"

"I promise Emmanuelle" pledged the long-jumper back on nimble feet, preparing to once more scurry across *British Style* garden to make another impressive wide leap. It was obvious to any listener the child wasn't just loyally repeating her teacher, or, providing rote-answers drummed so often into her young brain she instinctively parroted them with no thought as to what the words meant. No. Albertine spoke from her energetic, free-spirited heart. "Zebras might actually be really white with black stripes. I must investigate alone, personally seek out the truth and not merely believe what I'm told. As you taught me, Michel de Montaigne wrote: *Que-sais-je.*"

"Ooh-we!" young athlete squealed, sailing in properly-trained legs-first manner. If almost decade younger than Pascale, her own jet-black hair much shorter, Albertine was already four inches taller.

"Bravo, bravo Mlle. Albertine! Awesome Mlle. Albertine! Awesome, Mlle. Albertine!" cried Miniature Artist, clapping with all ladylike-enthusiasm. Not just in approval of her sister's budding-intellectual gifts, prodigious scholarship, but in praise of junior friend's latest bound. "Just as I taught and you so eagerly give it personal, Michel de Montaigne wrote: *Que-sais-je.* A girl should *know* not just *believe* she can succeed in a man's world through her own independent, positive, reasoned conclusions. She should *know* not just *believe* she doesn't need a man telling her what to do, even when she's got a skinned-knee."

"Yes Emmanuelle!" added Albertine, promptly getting up from where she landed on small fanny, dusting clothes off and walking back to line designated to start running to build up momentum for her next lunge. "We girls must think for ourselves, make use to the full of our own mental gifts, talents.

"Skinned knees" she said, "needn't reduce us to *Witless Women.* It's by thinking for ourselves even with skinned-knees that makes, we girls demonstrate we're just as good as, maybe even *better* than boys. It's by acting upon our own talents, rational judgments that we become creative, productive, worthwhile souls before God rather than pretty *Airheads,* just tape-recorders for scoundrels with trousers. Merely chattering parrots, or two-dimensional figures in pictures others draw of us. What did Descartes write? Cogitator ergo sum."

"Bravo! *I think therefore I am*"

"Here we go again, Emmanuelle" announce the long jumper speeding off again.

"And what did Simone Weil say, Mlle. Albertine?"

"Simone Weil" answered Albertine, appropriately in mid-air on the way to her best leap to date "Simone Weil wrote: 'I *act*, therefore I am.'"

III

"Do you miss your country, Emmanuelle?" queried the other twin: Marie, hesitantly, after first hurling far, next javelin. Throwing it so hard and with such energy, the girl stumbled forward a few steps after spear's release. Mme. de Charpentier was again abroad on a *UNICEF* mission. Vague but growing, persistent, rumors of terrorist attacks soon to occur in Paris, she last week dispatched her twins and their *Bunny Rabbit* to the seclusion of the family's isolated country estate in the French Alps. "Do you miss your country Emmanuelle? I've long wondered." At an altitude of over ten thousand feet above sea level, javelins sailed far in the fresh, cool, dry, low oxygen mountainous air.

"Yes, I do miss my country, Mlle. Marie" responded Pascale. A warm, comradely smile, intimate, reassuring voice signaling she wasn't upset the subject was mentioned; in fact, quite the opposite. "I know I'm French now and my, life is, now in France, but I can't help missing the place where I was born." She clapped enthusiastically upon seeing the exceptionally wide distance the javelin traveled.

"I'd feel unhappy too if I couldn't go home."

So kind of you, Mlle. Marie."

"Being an exile is supposed to be romantic, Emmanuelle. At least so it's said in novels, movies, poems and operas."

"Yes"

"Yes but is only romantic in novels, movies, poems and operas" supplied Marie, both in demonstration of sympathy and in indication she long prepared for the possible negative consequences of asking question. "It must a very nice place, though. Otherwise I wouldn't be so worried speaking of it in your presence, Emmanuelle, so worried I might make you cry."

Next, setting down spears, Marie took up bow and quiver. Instantly and in single, unified, well-honed motion, the child removed an arrow from the quiver, concentrated all outset of puberty attention on the target straight ahead across the sward paralleled by craggy peaks. She raised her bow pulled back the string, released.

Wish, Zap, Bull's-eye

Sibling Rivalry, on occasion and when waged by appropriate contestants can lead to positive results. "I'm not going to sit back and allow that silly, full-of-herself, no-sense-of-humor, ivory tower Albertine capture all the glory!" growled her twin silently. "I'm not going to let head-in-the-clouds Albertine, think I can't be in the *Olympics* too! Albertine might be able to win one gold medal but I'm going to win two! Just let's see if Albertine can ever match that!"

Wish, Zap, Bull's-eye

Off shot yet another arrow swift, high, sure and above all, far.

Wish, Zap, Bull's-eye

A third, fourth, fifth and sixth arrow sailed.

Additional *Wishes, Zaps, Bull's-eyes*

The archer appeared ancient mythology's Diana—the bold, independent, virgin huntress who champions girls who dare. Her courage; fleet, nimble foot; skill at personally mastering the chase; eagle-eyed feminine aim at all chosen prey far superior to that of all males

31

both divine and mortal, including her brother Apollo. Today, instead of she clad in traditional animal skins, barefoot, her long hair waving free in fresh breeze, virgin Diana wore a Roman Catholic schoolgirl uniform and mary-janes; her hair wound in pigtails tied with ribbons.

Additional: *Wishes, Zaps, Bull's-eyes*

"Bless you for all your concern about my feelings, Mlle. Marie!" thanked older girl much grateful, applauding ladylike and with deep maternal pride the grand example set by the archer's skill. "However I believe I got over the worst of that: *Scatterbrains, Knock, knock nobody Home, Weaker Sex* nonsense the day I also got over the side of the Pont Neuf and landed in the Hotel Dieu." She'd no desire elaborating on the most embarrassing incident in her life and the goddess of the hunt provided, guessed Pascale, a sanitized account of the disgraceful incident, didn't press for details.

"Good, good, I'm so relieved, Emmanuelle!" said virgin huntress Diana, providing affectionate peck on Pascale's right cheek. If originally found as a half-naked, starving orphan barely surviving off eating trash in an obscure Laotian jungle hamlet, the older of Raymonde's twins, could now conduct herself with faultless personal grace. One day she would surely become both an Olympic gold medalist (possibly in two events) and a more than worthy successor to the title of *Mme. de Charpentier.*

"Now please tell me more about where you come from, Emmanuelle. Please Emmanuelle dearest, tell me about where you once called home!"

"Are you sure, Mlle. DMarie? If I agree I might go on-and-on-and-on and still on-more" advised Pascale, her needy, indebted blush and suppressed giggle belying warning and any claim of reluctance telling the tale. "Sure? I've got so many fond memories about home once I start describing it I might not be able to stop."

Wish, Zap, Bull's-eye

"Please, please, Emmanuelle, go on-and-on-and-on-and-still-on-more. Tell me everything Emmanuelle. Tell me for hours! Please!"

"Alright"

When finally relating the facts of her severed-innocence, only fond, sweet thoughts arose in Pascale's adolescent, feminine consciousness.

First, she lovingly discussed Pierrette, Francoise and Agnes, her fellow Musketeers-in-bobby socks. Next, recounted riding upon her pony Penelope. Most of all, *Chere Petite* spoke expansively of her many adventurers with infinitely wise Father. As for those extended, unrequested encounters with middle-aged selected-groom, on this particular morning, Field Marshal Chamoun might as well for Pascale have never existed.

"Yes, yes tell me more, Emmanuelle" urged virgin huntress-Diana after friend described her past for over an hour. "Tell me more! For me a chance to listen is Awesome! No *really* awesome! Every detail! Did girls in your country too throw javelins? Did they too practice archery? Since we first met I've been dying to ask but felt uncertain I should raise the subject."

Wish, Zap, Bull's-eye

"Well, to begin with" recommenced Pascale, hugging friend with quiver now empty, tight.

IV

"Excellent job, girls!"

"Thank-you, Emmanuelle."

"Now it's time I start you two on *this* book."

"There are no pictures in this book?"

"I decided you girls are both good enough now not to need pictures."

V

"Are all we girls strapped-in? Is Mlle. Julienne fastened in the baby-seat?" questioned Pascale anxiously to young charges (in recent months expanded to three) as group scrambled into spacious, beige-color, leather second row of long, sleek, shiny, black stretch limousine. Normally, La Duchesse was driven by Ibrahim, a muscular, towering Algerian chauffeur, 40 bullet-clip semiautomatic at belt. However, since adopting

33

a third daughter last April in the Philippines, this one only weeks old, Ibrahim's dainty employer at times insisted taking own genteel control of the wheel, so as better persuade herself she exercising sufficient parental responsibility. Seated just beside La Duchesse, Pascale asked question from the front row.

"Yes, we are, Emmanuelle!" piped the Twins in unison. "Yes, little Julienne is fastened in her baby-seat!"

"Mlle. Marie, leave Mlle. Albertine alone!" swiftly reprimanded Pascale.

The feisty pair were at-battle again.

"Albertine hit me first!" accused one in canary yellow dress.

"I did not!" retorted twin in parakeet blue.

"You did *too.*"

"I'm going to throw-away all your bows and arrows, Marie!"

"If you do Albertine, I'll make-sure the whole world thinks you cheat at long jump! It's a baby-event too, made only for babies!"

"Long jump isn't a baby-event! It's the best event! Archery is for babies!"

"Is *not!*"

"*Is too!*"

"Watch-out!" snapped Pascale. "Watch-out or neither you brats will ever again be permitted modeling in my frescoes!"

"But Emmanuelle, Emmanuelle!" instantly begged Twins in humble, penitent unison. "You've already chosen us to appear in the fresco you started painting of Christ entering Jerusalem."

"I can easily white you two out and start-over again with better-behaved children as models!"

"I need to go to the toilet, Emmanuelle."

"Hurry up then! And do you too need going? If so, go now. We won't be able stopping again for over an hour."

"Do I *really* have to go on this trip, Emmanuelle?"

"Yes! And you'll enjoy it when you get there. History isn't a bunch of dates. It's our 'story. The most exciting 'story there is. I, guarantee very soon you'll think so too."

VI

"Wait, wait!" cried the younger Charpentier daughters as professional photographer was about to take official studio portrait of the family. "Let's, not leave our Emmanuelle out-of-the-picture!"

VII

"yes, yes! Go on, Emmanuelle. You know it!"

"Voi ch'ascoltate in rime sparse il suono"

"Told you so!"

"Di quei sospiri ond'io nudriva 'l core'"

Pascale spoke aloud in Italian, reciting from memory a Fourteenth Century sonnet written by Petrarca to Laura.

"Go on Mistress's treasure!" coaxed Raymonde. "You know it Sweetheart!"

"–In sul mio primo giovenile errore –"

"Yes, yes, Mistress's un-meddled-with own darling!"

"––Quand'era in parte altr'uom da quel ch'i' sono–"

"Wonderful! Wonderful! Magnificent!"

Two special friends wore identical, sleeveless, frilly, ivory-colored nightgowns. The uniquely: splendid curves, ever-so lovely lines, matchless touches of light and shadow comprising both Raymonde's fully-developed, and Pascale's own fine-blossoming teenage feminine body, were easily visible beneath thin, delicate material just barely covering each one of pair's graceful figure.

"–Del vario stile in ch'io piango et ragiono–"

The two buddies sat alone atop huge, multi-shade, intricately-designed Persian rug in palace's first floor *Louis XV Style* drawing room. High above, on forty-five-foot ceiling with Neoclassical moldings was a *Baroque* fresco by Watteau portraying Antony and Cleopatra cruising the Nile. Closer to earth, on the ducal chamber's four elegantly papered-walls hung life-size portraits of historic Charpentier ancestors. They, dressed either in armor; knee breeches, wigs; corsets, hoop-skirts;

mitered-cardinal's robes; abbess's habit and crozier. Their Images the work of Durer, Holbein, Poussin, De la Tour, Greuze.

"There's still a little bit more, Emmanuelle" was Raymonde's giggling, her fetching, happy face exhibiting a wide exuberant, girlish grin. To any outsider, this merry duo might be assumed fond classmates at a sleep-over party. To provide further encouragement, illustrate still more rightful pride in her special friend's phenomenal memory and good literary taste, Raymonde stood up. Long, thick, sinuous, coffee-and-cream colored hair in fetching face, La Duchesse clapped with all permissible ladylike fury. She jumped-and-down in place with all the energy considered acceptable for a member of so exclusive, rarefied a social circle. Patter of her genteel bare feet was muffled by Persian rug.

"–Fra le vane speranze e 'l van dolore –"

"Excellent, excellent, you God-given creature! Not that much more to go Angel, I've all the confidence in-the-world about you! Only one line left, Bunny Rabbit!"

"Che quanto piace al mondo e breve sogno."

Brilliant, Dear, how always so learned is Mistress's junior-Pompadour!"

Exhausted, out-of-breath, heart speeding, Raymonde plopped back on huge, multicolored, intricately designed Persian rug. Hair obscuring face, limbs weary.

"I so much enjoy Petrarca" informed Pascale after special friend recovered breath, pace of heart returned to normal. "The Middle Ages produced some really awesome poets."

"Those Dark Ages weren't as totally dark as people think, were they?"

"One day I'd like to visit Avignon and actually see where Petrarca met Laura."

"I'll be delighted taking you to Avignon, Sweetheart" promised Raymonde. "In fact, we'll make a week of it! We'll visit Arles, Provence, Nimes, the Roman ruins, too. Maybe, Carcassonne, as well. What about next month? Tommy will be away at another of his interminable-summits and the National Chamber of Deputies will be on summer recess. I'll have one of my all-too-few, too-rare vacations. We girls can go, then. Just you and me!"

"Yes Mistress! Just the two of us! Just the two of us alone together!"

"In meantime, let me kiss you again, hold you long and tight."

VIII

These and similar beloved memories from last two years paraded gently through teenage consciousness one lazy summer afternoon. If hardly composing tale for grand Italian opera, Pascale reflected, her unspectacular, unremarkable new life still brought each and every day precious humdrum reward, matchless commonplace fulfillment. While not as dramatic as *Tosca* leaping from the battlements or *Madame Butterfly* committing hare-kiri, assignment playing the roles of Duchess Charpentier's adoring protégée and of wise, protective *Big Sister* to Delphine, Albertine, now also Julienne, provided "Our Emmanuelle" incalculable emotional benefit.

"Goodness, gracious me!" she cried, jumping from oak four poster bed after checking wrist-watch. "Goodness, gracious, me!"

"'You and I shouldn't contemplate our-lives-away Emmanuelle" often advised Albertine—*The Little Philosopher.* "'Meditation is fine but if we don't look-out there' ll be no time left to act on your thoughts!'"

Straightening blouse, skirt, Pascale slipped-on pair of heels. After brushing jet-black mane in front of door-height closet mirror, she placed atop her head a wide-brimmed chapeau. Finally, taken from armchair a paperback copy of a novel she was currently reading, she sped down the stairs. "Goodness, gracious, time's a-wasting!"

"Off to meditate in the park again?" inquired Raymonde. Commandingly-elegant as ever, she watered hosts of roses, bougainvilleas, salvias, orchids, carnations, hydrangeas and blossoming rhododendrons, crocus set in oriental vases near front door.

"Yes, Mistress"

"Mistress is attending a ceremony in two hours and taking *Bunny Rabbit* along to provide company. This event will also enable her *Bluebird* to be free from the children a little while."

Pascale gestured questioningly toward her clothes.

"Oh, you look quite lovely as you are, darling" assured the Olympian, pecking favorite toy's red painted lips. "Besides, it's not one of those *hoity-toity* groups. They're serious-minded, like, you! Perhaps you'll make a friend!"

"I'll be delighted, then, Mistress!"

PENSIVE AFTERNOON

$\mathcal{P}$ascale exited the Métro at *Palais Royal*, emerging on Rue Rivoli, paralleling the Louvre. Before crossing to south side of this fashionable, seeming forever traffic-congested thoroughfare in central Paris, she devoted a half-hour to avid widow-shopping the arcades giving this particular underground transport stop its name.

During the later Eighteenth Century prior to 1789, Philippe "Egalité" Duc d'Orléans, leader of the cadet-branch of the Bourbon Dynasty, cousin and rival to Louis XVI, maintained his seat in the capital at the Palais Royal—the most famous in this multifaceted archipelago of *Baroque* and *Neoclassical* structures consisting of: upscale residential homes, ministerial offices; a stock exchange, national library and bank;,renowned theater; commercial space and lovely, shady thought-provoking, quadrangles. An egotistical self-promoter, political adventurer, spendthrift, womanizer—Philippe "Egalité" was constantly short of cash. As one means of securing its steady-flow, he rented much of the ground floor of his palace's unused south wing to merchants. If the Revolution eventually sent their landlord to the guillotine, his tenants survived. In time, the rented-out south wing of the Palais Royal complex with its shopping arcades facing Rue Rivoli paralleling the Louvre became synonymous with ladies fashion.

"I wonder if Duchess Charpentier will ever permit me to also wear *those*" whispered her loyal sidekick plaintive, once more gazing long and yearning through the front plate-glass window of a prestigious, exclusive boutique situated beneath the Palais Royal arcades. Offered for purchase within were the apex of chic, daring French lingerie and the unchallengeable summit of flirtatious, exotic stockings. No prices were shown—clear indication that for the elite feminine clientele serviced by Mademoiselle Eveline and Mademoiselle Celeste, the ever-stylishly-dressed, coiffured owners of rarefied establishment, cost was no object. Even merest passing-thought of money was considered by those entering famous shop, the epitome of loudmouth-American tourist, parvenu, social-climber vulgarity.

"I wonder, if Duchess Charpentier will ever permit me to also wear *those*?" repeated her little protégée again in frantic, yearning whisper. "Duchess Charpentier wears *those* every day, wears only *those*. In fact, Duchess Charpentier wouldn't quite be—*Duchess Charpentier*—if not every day wearing only *those*. And she's the most awesome lady who ever lived and ever *will* live! It makes me so awesomely-glad when Mistress is pleased with me—when Mistress approves of what I do or say! I want to be just like her!" Then, after scolding self for sin of envy, added: "not that I could ever hope being anywhere near as awesome a lady as her! All the same, I must-must-must try my very best to be like Mistress! And if I'm going to try my very best to be like Mistress, I've got to wear *those*!"

Pascale straightened her socks.

"But I can't wear *those* without permission. I'm sure if I go about it the right way, Mistress might just possibly grant it. But I've got to go about it the right way, find the proper time and place to ask permission." *Ask permission*—continued a frequently-employed phrase in Songbird's speech.

Adolescent face and hands pressed intently against the plate-glass window. Enraptured-teenage gray-green eyes surveyed and youthful mind contemplated being at last able to wear chic, daring lingerie, flirtatious, exotic stockings. Just four-foot-ten inches tall, this girl, even in heels, needed rising on tip-toes for a better glimpse within boutique itself. The big sister smiles and motions of sympathetic acknowledgment she received intermittently from Mademoiselle Eveline and Mademoiselle Celeste, demonstrated *Little Giotto* was to them not merely a familiar figure but also shop mascot. One, whom, the two elegant merchants frequently invited inside for tea and cookies.

In truth, this celebrated boutique first captured Pascale's rapt, undiminished imagination before she even knew Raymonde existed! The youngster's original encounter with the magical place occurred while still assuming she must return home in less than a week to marry Field Marshal Chamoun! Since that day, Pascale never failed if she in central Paris to gaze long and hopeful through this enchanting window.

Father and Field Marshal Chamoun, as *Chere Petite* knew well, would never once consent to she wearing chic, daring, lingerie and flirtatious, exotic stockings. While the leaders of the Francophone, pro-Western, military regime formerly controlling Pascale's birthplace were determined transforming it into a modern, industrialized, secular state and undisputed regional military/economic-power, they also studiously avoided offending the deeply conservative cultural traditions of country's large Arabic-speaking, Muslim-majority. Among this category of social customs deemed off-limits to government interference, was the Muslim dress code for women.

As a practicing-Roman Catholic, daughter of the Minister of Defense and fiancée of her country's Prime Minister, Pascale never was forced into dressing as an anonymous worker-ant, slavish drone-bee, or indistinguishable member of vast termite colony. Neither, however, was she allowed to openly flaunt majority cultural tradition. Miniskirts, sleeveless blouses (except at public events), high heels—she was allowed. Chic, daring, feminine undergarments—she was *not*.

When first pressing her teenage nose and hands intently against the plate glass window of this Parisian boutique on Rue Rivoli, *Chere Petite* knew a wish was only a wish. Two eventful and formative years later—no longer in Paris as a tourist, she now frequently invited inside the boutique by its owners to share tea, cookies, *Girl-talk*—previous *wish* appeared about to become reality. The warm, affectionate gestures Mademoiselle Eveline and Mademoiselle Celeste offered little friend served to only further confirm their mascot's desperate hope.

"Awesome! No, *really, really* awesome!"

Filled with indescribable excitement, Pascale eagerly returned the pretty merchants' waves and smiles. Each motion she made from just outside the window humbly expressed immense gratitude for her adult friends' continued affection and understanding.

"Time I'm off" *Chere Petite* decided at last, "or I'll have no time reading before Mistress comes for me."

Throwing kisses, offering them silent words of love, Pascale signaled Mademoiselle Eveline and Mademoiselle Celeste goodbye. Scurrying across Rue Rivoli as fast as heels permitted, she next advanced westward along the opposite side of the thoroughfare until reaching an opening to the wide outer western quadrangle of the Louvre with its distinctive, glass pyramid and triumphal *Baroque* arch. Traveling still on at steady, assured, optimistic, refined gait, Pascale at last approached the Tuilleries Gardens at far end the Place de Concorde. She was meticulous to deliver some of the life-size female statues near the park's east opening a polite wave of recognition.

I

Some minutes later, Pascale settled ladylike upon a comfortable green wooden bench beneath a shade-bestowing, centuries-witnessing oak. This time of year all the woods in this historic garden formed a single orchestra of brightly colored-growth. Voices of unseen songbirds on gently-swaying higher branches further contributing to the sense of living nature's symphonic omnipresence. Once, while visiting the Musée d'Orsay, she recalled observing a beautiful canvas depicting a similar aged-girl located on what appeared the very same green wooden bench under the identical oak, girl was seated today!

"Who was the painter?" had long wondered Pascale both day and night. Her continued, nagging inability recalling the painter's name sometimes led to loss of sleep. "What was her name?"

Yes, it was a *female* artist, definitely—one, among the just handful to win lasting fame and wide critical respect during the male-dominated period they lived. Not that most women were then lacking in creative talent. Rather, the snooty art conservatories of the time refused to accept girls as students. Girls were welcome to enter so men could paint or sketch them nude but not in order to perfect their own artistic talent and certainly not permitted in to paint men naked.

The female painter's illusive name was distinct in Adolescent mind's eye. The name began with the same letter as a number of her contemporaries.

"Perhaps that's why it's so difficult to remember?"

She and the other artists with whom she is associated with her are today labeled as members of the same school of painting. Viewed as iconoclastic at the time, their work vehemently denounced by the social powers-that-be as mediocre, crude, even pornographic, their work is now a central pillar of French cultural identity.

It was with the hope of both locating the spot recorded in the canvas and of curing her insomnia that Pascale first entered this enjoyable garden running parallel the Right Embankment west of the Louvre. Following extensive library research and photographic comparisons, *there* it was—same tree; same gravel walkway; identical public fountain just ahead! So much for the supposed ravages inflicted by time and human events! Except for whimsical alterations in costume among passersby, the scene was completely unchanged since suddenly-forgotten-artist departed with her paints, canvas and easel.

"*Berthe Morisot!*" Pascale immediately piped, triumphant. "How could I ever be so silly as forgetting Berthe Morisot's name!"

Seeking-out the niche, finding it to be as pleasant as in the picture, she came here again, then again. By this current afternoon, the spot was become ha well-established venue for reading and reflection; a blessed haven for quiet thought amidst an impersonal, fast-paced modern world. She was surrounded by a glorious abundance of colorful wisteria, rambling roses, gladiolas, hollyhocks, snapdragons, tulips, petunias, zinnias, delphiniums, morning glories, iris and orchids.

Pascale opened her dog-eared paperback, turning to the page left-off the previous evening. Fluent since childhood in multiple foreign languages, she didn't require a French translation of Thomas Hardy's *Tess of the d'Urbervilles.*

"It's so unfortunate" the young reader speculated Pascale after a few minutes, "so unfortunate that girls as intelligent, brave and single-minded as Tess arise only in literature! These fictional heroines are never taken-in by the absurd excuses far more politically-advantaged, far better-educated flesh-and-blood girls casually accept from males. What's it that attracts so many girls to men who're scoundrels, losers, hypocrites? What's it that drives them to desire only men who're cruel, unfaithful, egotistic? Generation after generation—it appears endemic among our sex."

Midpoint in the novel was just passed. If one might dimly perceive the climax ahead, its precise resolution was still tantalizingly unknown. "No surprise" observed the reader, "*Tess of the d'Urbervilles* was originally published in monthly magazine installments."

Pascale returned to her dog-eared paperback. Thomas Hardy was her favorite novelist.

Yet this afternoon for some inexplicable reason, the narrative wasn't as exciting. Strange, considering Tess was making a crucial decision!

Pascale adjusted her skirt.

Fiddled with angle of chapeau, fondled collar of sleeveless blouse.

Her right shoe tapped.

Bare legs crossed opposite.

Teenage gray-green eyes surveyed the same paragraph once, twice, a third time.

Words normally evoking unforgettable images of human struggle, today held interest only as eccentric, geometrical shapes.

"Lower-case *G*s are rather peculiar if one gives them thought!" Pascale mused. "Lower-case *B*s, resemble reverse, upside-down depictions of Africa. The Indian subcontinent, if one includes Pakistan and Bangladesh —Bangladesh used to be called East Pakistan —looks like a *V*."

"At what date" she furthered conjectured. "did Europeans abandon *Roman Numerals* for *Arabic Numbers*? The latter are far more practical. Try multiplying MDLXXIX by CCCXXVIII? Goodness, gracious me! Likely the change wasn't before the *Crusades* beginning in 1096. Of course I'm no authority. Father would know. Father knows everything!"

After ten minutes of mental roaming, *Chere Petite* set the dog-eared paperback aside. Rising to feet, she paced in a wide circle, her arms behind back with clasped wrists, pensive head tilted slightly down in Napoleonic pose.

PHOTO-OPPORTUNITY

....

"*Still* debating *The-meaning-of-Life*?" called a melodious familiar voice. "Still contemplating your proper place in *The-grand-scheme-of-Things*?"

Beneath ocean of hair, Pascale turned about, swiftly.

"Mistress's *Robin Redbreast* has developed quite a reputation in our neighborhood as a philosopher, theologian, a pretty 'King Solomon in all his, *her* 'wisdom.'" remarked Raymonde, tender. Approaching gracefully from tree-shaded path on the left, she wore a white, short, silk, spaghetti-straps dress, natural pearls around her sculpted neck, on ears; Edith Wharton Era-chapeau; obscenely-expensive Italian spiked-heels. Her delicate right bare arm was lifted to push-back the low-hanging branch of a chestnut tree, left, clutched *Hermes Birkin* handbag. "What with your serious reading, pacing, pensive expression, only vaguest description was needed for several passersby to immediately provide Mistress directions for retrieving her most valuable property. 'Oh, of course Madame La Duchesse, you must be referring to *The Deep Thinker*. Just make a left."

Pascale was deeply embarrassed, body squirmed.

The Olympian came, to the girl's swift assistance.

"Don't fear *Songbird*. The world needs more innocent, noble spirits like you!" assured Madame La Duchesse de Charpentier-Martignac.

She pecked her awestruck protégée on the lips, offered her little disciple a queenly bare arm. "It's time we two ladies go? Now take Mistress's arm!"

46

Pascale gripped the chatelaine's arm tight with both hands.

She rubbed own adolescent cheek humbly, reverent, longingly against her heroine's unblemished, firm, smooth, soft, cool skin.

"I hope finding me didn't cause inconvenience, Mistress? I hope it didn't make you go far-off your route?"

"Not at all Sweetheart, Mistress is going this direction anyway. Don't forget to bring Thomas Hardy along!"

After returning *Tess of the d'Urbervilles* to her handbag, Pascale again desperately gripped Raymonde's arm; she once more rubbed teenage cheek reverently on heroine's unblemished, firm, smooth, soft, cool skin.

"What precisely are we attending, Mistress?"

"You've heard of Sister Jeanne Navarro?"

"Yes, of course, Mistress. I've never met Sister Jeanne but I know all about her."

"Of course you know of her, *Songbird*. You know about Sister Jeanne through Véronique and her brother Richard, through your special friends Sister Claire and Sister Genevieve. The devout pair belong to Sister Jeanne's order of social-activist, feminist nuns. They look to Sister Jeanne as their Superior."

"I've always wanted meeting Sister Jeanne. Sister Jeanne must be an awesome lady. Not as awesome as you of course, Mistress!"

"Straighten your socks, *Robin Redbreast*. History isn't made by girls who don't straighten their socks!"

I

Awaiting at the eastern mouth of the Tuilleries Gardens near the large, *Neoclassical,* female statues each representing a major French province was parked Raymonde's long, sleek, shiny, black, armored stretch limousine with clouded, bullet-proof windows. A United Nations pennant was mounted on each of the vehicle's four corners. It carried UN license plates a, communications antennae mounted at the left rear guaranteed riders immediate and confidential access to all the *powers-that-be*. Raymonde and her protégée climbed into a cozy passenger compartment with beige leather seat and thick white carpet. It sported too, a color television, movie screen, *CD*-player, liquor bar, refrigerator-freezer, computer, high-frequency radio, telephone. Raymonde's handsome, athletic, six-foot-six-inch, Algerian, liveried chauffeur speaking perfect French, a 40 bullet-clip semiautomatic at his belt, took wheel.

"Rose, are you and your assistant safely buckled-in?" asked Ibrahim. "I'll not proceed until the two ladies are safely buckled-in." His words were instantly recognizable beneath their aloof, bureaucratic delivery as warm, loving, intimate and protective. This former highly-decorated French Foreign Legion paratroop colonel served as Mme. de Charpentier's social-chief-of-staff, appointment's-secretary, unofficial-diplomatic envoy, armed-bodyguard and personal chauffeur since the Lisbon Games. Much closer in age to his distinguished charge than were Uncle and Auntie to their niece Mary Preston, the immense affection Ibrahim possessed for Mme. de Charpentier instead of parental was of another kind.

"Yes faithful, loyal, far-nobler-soul-than-Rose-will-ever-possibly-be, we are, Ibrahim" replied elegant, pretty, ultra-chic employer.

"Good" answered Ibrahim, protectively, "off-we-go. Despite all the traffic, I know a side route which can get Rose to her destination well in time."

The sleek, shiny, black, armored stretch limousine with *UN* markings sped-off. Policemen on motorcycles, two behind, two in front, accompanied.

"Maybe on the way home you'd like seeing a film, Sweetheart?" suggested Raymonde, gesturing with free arm her protégée inspect wide selection of *VHS* and DVDs in easy reach. "There're sure to be at least six or seven here which you would certainly enjoy watching. Mistress sees all the new ones even before they reach the theaters."

"Yes, thank-you Mistress for being so kind and generous!" eagerly answered Pascale, her adolescent eyes bedazzled, she exhibiting further teenage enrapture by repeatedly patting hands atop own thighs. "Yes indeed Mistress, I'll be delighted to watch a film on return!"

"Good. In meantime we'll listen to some music" informed Raymonde wearing a short, tailored, silk, strapless dress. Inserting a collection of John Field sonatas into the *CD*-player, she then she then allowed Pascale to desperately, beseeching, kissed heroine's bare shoulders. Briefly wriggling free to recover her protégée's chapeau, Raymonde again permitted she be fervently embraced, be gratefully clutched and reverently kissed. When at last out of breath, Pascale rested her head on heroine's left bare shoulder.

The beautiful piano sonatas of John Field embraced car's entire passenger compartment. Pascale and Raymonde closed their eyes. Soon, both were conscious only of the pair's mutual, intimate presence,. Tey permitted time to fondly pass. Beyond the clouded, bullet-proof windows of the armored stretch limousine with diplomatic markings, the hectic, violent, impersonal world continued surging on its cold, lonely, often unproductive, unfriendly way. For the two ladies traveling inside the vehicle there was only peace, gentleness and love.

SCREECH

A mid-forties American tourist couple—each in western boots, Niemann-Marcus post-Christmas 50%-off Sale attire, *Dallas Cowboys* jersey, Stetson; the woman: a fake-blond with mammoth earrings, push-up brazier, gaudy jewelry, too-much makeup and too little space in polyester pants to comfortably enclose expanding stomach, overloaded *Galleries Lafayette* hopping-bag grasped in each her avaricious-hands— suddenly darted forward. Although traffic light visibly against them, the couple scampered merrily across boulevard. The two escaped being run-over, totally crushed beneath huge armored stretched limousine, only when Ibrahim just in time slammed foot on breaks.

SCHREECH

As reward for saving human lives, he was shown two self-righteous middle fingers. Receiving also, from the fake-blond in polyester, contents of her overloaded *Galleries Lafayette* shopping bags now scattered on pavement, a torrent of curses spoken in English.

"Idiot Americans!" growled Ibrahim. "They should finally understand they *don't* own the world, are *not* the summit of all human achievement! Americans should finally realize the rest of the world and its inhabitants *weren't* created to merely tell them *Yes Milord, Yes Milady.* Or, pander to America and to American's every idle, vulgar, materialist, grasping whim!"

"Ah! Ah!" cried Raymonde from the row behind, genteel. The sudden deafening screech of limousine's tires, abrupt, strong jolt of its heavy armored chassis startled the passengers out of mutual, fond semi-sleep.

"Are you hurt, Rose?" asked Ibrahim, frantic. "Are you injured, Rose? I'll come to your assistance at once! Don't be frightened! I'm coming to save you, Rose!"

"Oh! Oh!" the damsel cried, breathless. "Your weak, vulnerable Rose is in desperate need! Your gentle, fragile Rose needs rescue! If Ibrahim doesn't come at once to protect his fair lady will—"

She collapsed.

Not fainted at all, Raymonde momentarily opened her eyes to deliver her protégée a signal she hastily withdraw to far side of spacious, beige limousine passenger compartment. Pascale at once obeyed. At her small size, the chamber seemed even larger than it already was. Having attained that distant shore, contracted her nicely-developing four-foot-ten feminine body into erect fetal position—legs held tight against torso with hands at ankles, chin rested atop knees—Little Giotto closely observed.

Quickly, Ibrahim exited the driver's seat door. After making threatening gesture toward his 40 bullet-clip semiautomatic to disperse curious approaching pedestrians, he threw open the left passenger compartment door. There, he discovered his lovely employer in midst of a *Victorian*-melodrama, grand Italian opera swoon.

If still secure atop her head thanks to hatpins, Raymonde's fashion-setting chapeau was now rendered smartly out-of-place; long coffee-and-cream color hair pushed stylishly, skew. The string of natural pearls around her sculpted-neck was driven awry, voguish. Collapsing in a tailored, short, silk, strapless dress, additional inches of her celebrated lower limbs were visible; already memorable cleavage yet expanded. Meticulous to fall neatly across beige leather seat rather than sprawl ungainly on car floor with legs spread, dress torn; she assured her privates were concealed, her shapely breasts not fully uncovered. Similarly, instead of it dropping from grip as a swooning lady might usually lose her purse: spewing makeup, fragrance and other contents, the *Hermes Birkin* handbag remained snapped shut, seated atop its owner's lap. She didn't break a heel.

Lying comfortable in tastefully-erotic pose, sensual but not indecent, seeming unconscious, Raymonde gradually convalesced from dignified faint.

As Raymonde's lungs appeared to re-inhale lost oxygen, heart reestablishibg normal beat, her bust once more rose and fell precisely at the gentle, relaxed rhythm expected of a pious Grand Lady. One, who just narrowly escaped collision with vulgar Americans seeking to interfere with her performance of selfless, Christian, "good works." As for the incident causing her prolonged "fragile female" swoon, this too was fully in accordance with popular custom. Also true to form, she apparently only after a, few minutes, awoke.

"That, Emmanuelle, is how it's, done!" indicated Raymonde's wink to sidekick. "That, Emmanuelle, is how it's done! Mind you observe carefully! In time Mistress will demand as good a performance from you!"

"Are you injured, Rose?" pleaded Ibrahim, on his knees.

"No Ibrahim" chatelaine answered, still breathless, fluttering her eyelids, offering a vulnerable, shaking right hand for him to instantly clutch with both own, provide it many heartfelt kisses.

"Thank God Rose" answered chauffeur, still on knees, still clutching proffered hand tight. At last, releasing own right hand, he then slowly, lovingly, stroked his employer's hair. "Thank God you're not injured, Rose."

"Ibrahim, my champion," she answered, breathless, fluttering her eyelids.

No fool, even in love, Ibrahim wasn't taken-in. Increasingly fewer opportunities arising since start of Raymonde's diplomatic career for pair to be alone, to be close, enjoy private, extended physical contact, Ibrahim, 40 bullet-clip semi-automatic at belt, was eager continuing this charade. "Thank God, you're uninjured my Rose!"

"Yes, Ibrahim."

He and dainty passenger joined eyes confiding, understanding, sympathetic.

Their lips exchanged smiles of recognition.

Two breathed in one fond accord.

A moment passed, second elapsing.

Raymonde let Ibrahim stroke her sheerest hosed-legs.

"No, no, your Rose isn't hurt," she assured tender, deferential; allowing chauffeur better inspection of his employer's cleavage. "Nor hurt is Mademoiselle Emmanuelle. We ladies are simply a bit shaken-up. But thanks so-so much being anxious. Your Rose never feels as warm, safe, secure as when she's in her hero's valiant, firm protection. Rose is confident that whatever happens from this day forth, she can always rely on a guide and defender."

He no fool even in love, Ibrahim, wasn't taken-in. All the same, with increasingly fewer opportunities since Raymonde began diplomatic career for the pair to be close, to enjoy extended, physical contact, Ibrahim was quite eager playing along with the charade.

"So tell me more about where you're taking me, Mistress" questioned Pascale after the limousine set-off again. She cuddled-up against Raymonde's side. "What am I going to be attending?"

"The announcement of the desired outcome to delicate peace negotiations"

"*Peace negotiations,* Mistress?"

"The announcement of their desired outcome, Dear!" reminded the Olympian in voice of justified pride, rightful sense of major personal accomplishment. She crossed her legs opposite.

"The: *hoped for outcome,* Mistress?"

"The leadership of two countries long at war finally sought peace" illuminated Raymonde, the *CD* recording of John Field piano sonatas now finished. "The general populations of these two countries though, weren't at all sure they wanted peace. Quite the reverse in fact! Why, for many of them, hating-your-neighbor long ago became a pillar of personal psyche, definition of an individual's sole reason for existence, sole purpose on earth. Human beings tend to feel safe, warm, confident when life meanders down a path set for them by others—when life is predictable, when there's no fear of sudden changes intervening to upset routine, no fear men and women might be forced to make use of God's gift to them of freewill."

"We're creatures-of-habit, Mistress"

"So indeed we are, Sweetheart" answered Raymonde, crossing her legs opposite. "In some ways humans are no superior in the Darwinian eat-or-be-eaten animal system than ants in an anthill, bees in a beehive or termites in termite mound."

"Mama doesn't agree, Mistress."

"Ah but that's precisely why Firebird wanted her Rose taking you in-hand" confided Raymonde, enigmatic. "But I digress" she continued. "Be they termites or angels, history clearly shows humans prefer routine. Even as we see in the Middle East, Afghanistan or central Africa for instance, what they look upon as safe, warm, confident, secure 'routine' is—murder and mayhem. So the leaders of the two countries seeking peace didn't want their efforts made public until a formal peace treaty could be announced. If it became known a peace overture is afoot earlier, influential portions of the population in both countries might actively seek to stop the peace process. If negotiations failed, leaders attempting them might be accused of being traitors."

"So each side's leader wished to present powerful opponents in his own respective ranks with a *fait accompli* like Nixon going to China or F.W. De Klerk releasing Nelson Mandela?" eagerly interpreted Pascale.

"Yes"

"An action which once done can't be undone, an action irrevocably setting the current order on its head. One, giving supporters of the status quo no alternative but making the best of a new state of affairs."

"Exactly so, you: Talleyrand-without-a-clubfoot; you: Churchill-who-doesn't-smoke-nasty-cigars; you Gladstone-in-a-skirt!"

Pascale looked away, embarrassed.

"And what was your role, Mistress?"

"Mistress was approached by representatives of both sides and informed of their efforts. She promptly made both her formal office and her private residence available for each side to send representatives without it being assumed they ever met each other. Also, without the press ever discovering what was up. Mistress both convened and led these mere 'idle talks,' 'off-the-record,' 'exploratory' chats, herself. Sometimes in downtown Paris, on other occasions while over tea at *Palais Charpentier.* In time, her hostessing, blushing, her salving of little boy egos succeeded in its purpose. More details as to Mistress's precise role she won't give you at this moment."

"You'll be able to give me more detail later?"

"Of course, *Robin Redbreast,* you'll be told the entire story. Mme. de Charpentier is a *Scatterbrained Female,* a witless woman chatterbox. She can never keep secrets."

"You're an *international diplomat,* Mistress!" admonished Pascale, unhappy with heroine's persistent self-denigration. "You're an awesome *international diplomat!*"

"When Mistress was your age" mused Raymonde, nostalgic, "she was speeding for hours around the cloister garden every day, Sister Madeleine in black habit, *Rosary* beads in one hand, stopwatch in other, crying 'Faster Rose, faster! That's not good enough! Put some effort into it! You've still another half-second to get-off if you're going to represent our convent at the Olympics!' Mistress already long yearned for a gold medal. But imagining she'd later one day be too, a diplomat? As you express it so well, it makes one feel—awesome!"

The long, sleek, shiny, armored black stretch limousine and motorcycle escort approached its final destination.

"See that wide unpainted-area, Emmanuelle?" instructed Raymonde, gesturing to large space above marble stairs leading to the front entrance of the office building limousine approached. "See that unpainted-area, *Bunny Rabbit.* If these negotiations are successful, their success will certainly deserve commemoration in a mural at the site the peace treaty was achieved. Until this moment all your murals are at Father Richard's church. All your brilliant frescoes are located off-the-beaten-track. The very existence of the New Arena Chapel is only known to a small number of individuals in a church rarely visited by tourists. It's time you create a public mural."

She again gestured to wide, unpainted space above marble stairs.

"I'm sure there are many artists who're far more experienced and closer-acquainted with such matters than me, Mistress!" begged-off *Chere Petite*, voluminous jet-black hair covering face. If long recovered from artistic block, the prospect of exhibiting her work outside the protective, loving environment of Richard's church, *La Nouvelle Heloise* and the Charpentier family's walled estate filled the girl with almost physically-painful dread. "I'm not good enough to be seen in public!"

"Nonsense, Emmamuelle! You're the best possible artist for the job! Mistress brought *Pet* along for more reasons than diplomatic escapades. Diplomacy in fact was only a pretext. Mistress made two pledges to Firebird when asked to take you in-hand. First, she pledged to cure you of your creative block, make you again a Little Giotto. This first pledge solemnly made to her dearest, closest, most cherished friend this side of heaven Mistress has fulfilled."

"However the second pledge" continued Raymonde, "is yet to be fulfilled. That's, to see Emmanuelle's artistic-brilliance known beyond the 5th and 16th Arrondissement. You must and Mistress says *must* exhibit to the General Public. Once a wider number of people in France appreciate your work it'll only be short time before your work is forever immensely appreciated, admired, honored, and even immensely *loved* by the entire planet! You're a genius, Child, the greatest painter to appear in centuries! You're a genius, the greatest painter to appear in centuries whether you like it or not! This gift cannot be wasted. You possess a *Vocation.* God is calling you to Him! God selected you as *The Messenger* and it's your purpose in life, place on earth to deliver the message!"

She held young companion close. "I possess immense social and cultural influence, Emmanuelle-treasure. Agree to exhibit and I'll take care of the rest. A genius like you shouldn't even be involved in tawdry business matters anyway. I'll see to it all. Just give the word."

Teenager cringed with agonizing self-doubt.

"Show my pictures to the public Mistress?"

"Yes, Sweetheart, just give the word! I'll see to the rest. No need you ever concern yourself with cheap, tawdry business matters. Put all cheap, tawdry business matters out of your simple, innocent, priceless little head. I'll see to all business arrangements."

"If you say so" answered Miniature Artist, noncommittal.

"In a few minutes my *Robin Redbreast*" instructed Raymonde, "you'll be introduced to a truly great man. The greatest man Firebird and I know. And believe me, over the last twenty years Firebird and I have been provided abundant opportunities to size-up gentlemen asserting to be *great*. We've each no trouble recognizing the difference between truth and falsehood. This truly great individual I'll introduce you is a scholar among scholars, an academician among academicians, poet among poets! He's a Christian among Christians!"

'Until I met His Eminence" she confided, "I secretly thought Christianity was only mumbo-jumbo, hocus-pocus. This brilliant gentleman is as truly spiritual as he's part of this world. He opened Christianity up to me! You don't need just attending a house of worship or reading the Bible to discover Christ. Just listen to the profound words of this gentleman you're about to be introduced! I know that after I tell him about you he'll agree with me. He too will insist: 'Child, you must give a public exhibition. This is the only way to proceed with the blessing God granted you.' Listen to him. He's wise man!"

"Mistress, you said Sister Jeanne Novarro will be present?" injected Pascale in lively, adolescent voice, determined she change unnerving subject of conversation. "I'm so-so excited to meet Sister Jeanne."

"Yes, she'll be present, *Songbird*. I knew that would entice *Pet* coming. Sister Jeanne and her disciples are today become to say the least 'influential' in our Roman Catholic community. There's none of that—'silent as a nun'—rule in the Order she established. Her Order is become influential today in more than cultural and social spheres too!"

Pascale wasn't uninformed about topic.

"As last autumn's parliamentary elections in Germany, Belgium, the Netherlands, Austria, Spain and Italy clearly show" observed Raymonde, "and as those last month here in France too demonstrate beyond dispute, Sister Jeanne exercises the pivotal constituency level-role in determining the outcome. One might even say it's because of Sister Jeanne that so many members of Tommy's party in the Chamber of Deputies now suddenly find themselves unemployed!"

"Wide swaths of deeply-religious, culturally-traditional, politically-conservative provincial voters" she recounted, "people normally not supporting the Left this side of God's creation did so last month anyway. Why? Because this time the proposed social agenda of the 'godless,' 'immoral' Left was delivered not by overbearing, condescending, *Slumming-it,* intellectuals shaking fists and wearing denim but instead advocated by sweet, young, idealistic nuns. My relatives were singing the praises of Sister Jeanne and her call for *True Socialism.* 'No wonder the capitalists wanted Jesus Christ eliminated!' my Gaullist mother told me. 'Jesus Christ supported the workers.'"

"Labor union paladins, long far more interested in competing with one another than representing the best interests of their rank-and-file membership" said Raymonde, "only agreed uniting behind a single Left candidate because the sisters' intervention allowed each union rival to withdraw his own claim to the candidacy without losing face, without appearing to surrender to a hated competitor."

"So it was essential for this afternoon's event" she summarized, "given the religious make-up of the two countries formerly at war, to have prominent representatives of the French Roman Catholic community at the ceremony. If she isn't attending there'll be more talk across Europe and the Middle East about Sister Jeanne not co-signing it than about the peace treaty itself."

"But we're Conservatives!" interjected Pascale, loyally. "We're Conservatives! I hope Mistress isn't too angry with Sister Jeanne for her role in making we Conservatives lose our rightful majority in the Chamber of Deputies?"

"Not at all Sweetheart!" chirped the Olympian. "No bad feelings at all! A thorough shake-up is the price our party needed to pay to acquire better, bolder leadership in the future. Tommy and his *Old Guard* cronies got exactly what was coming to them! The haughty, sexist asses! Pardon my unladylike-language."

"I kept pleading with Tommy" elaborated President Belanger's intimate companion, smile of just pride on her moist painted lips. "I kept pleading we Conservatives must reach an accommodation with Sister Jeanne. I kept warning Tommy we Conservatives shouldn't underestimate Sister Jeanne's influence at the polls, shouldn't underestimate her clout in the National Chamber of Deputies, or undervalue how many electoral districts her nuns can deliver. But did Tommy and his minions heed my warning, pay me any attention? Of, course not! I'm just a stupid woman. 'What-the-devil could Rose ever possibly know about politics?' Tommy and our party's *Old Guard* scoffed. 'What-the-devil could silly-Rose know about current affairs?' 'All flibbertigibbet-Rose can do is wear pretty dresses, look cute, run in a circle! 'She likely only got that appointment at the UN through sleeping with the right Israelite, Chinaman, or Nigger!' 'Why listen to *Scatterbrains*-Rose who can only wear pretty dresses, look cute and run in a circle.'"

"No, no faithful Emmanuelle darling" promised Raymonde. "I hold nothing at all against Sister Jeanne! In fact, I admire her. I *greatly* admire Sister Jeanne and her fellow nuns. Given my personal temperament, ambitions, if the circumstances of my birth, class position, childhood, upbringing had been different, I too might very well belong to Sister Jeanne's Order today! I'm secretly overjoyed seeing Tommy lose his majority in the Chamber of Deputies. Lose it so handily! Lose it so handily to women, too, even if those women are filthy Socialists."

"Yes, Mistress. Women are supposed to be Conservatives, not filthy Socialists."

Raymonde took Pascale to lips, held girl close, long, tender.

"But don't think you've engineered Mistress into setting aside your public art exhibition!" admonished La Duchesse, abruptly releasing companion, speech reverted to *Vous* aloof, *Third Person*. "You can't disobey Mistress that easily!"

II

Admitted through heavy police barricades sealing off access to the quiet square to all but a few previously designated cars and all pedestrians, the Duchess's long, sleek, shiny, armored stretch limousine with *UN* banners and markings, motorcycle escort accompanying, reached its destination. Two passengers emerged precisely in the manner ladies are meant to exit vehicles. A crowd of dignitaries was assembled for what looked to bw an historic ceremony. Several dozen dapper gents and their stylish dames were engaged in animated discussion. The group consisted of: politicos; diplomats in white tie, morning coat and striped pants; military commanders in full dress uniform; business leaders; members of the Académie Francaise; *NGO* directors, wealthy philanthropists, socially active, Left-leaning film stars; opera divas; and two foreign ambassadors careful to stand at the periphery so as not to overly draw attention them.

Snap, snap, snap, snap, additional camera snaps.

Paparazzi catering to sensationalist, mass-circulation, tabloid dailies or celebrity weekly magazines, snapped complicated Japanese gadgets at furious, nonstop pace. Independent contractors rather than salaried-employees, each was paid up to 50,000 *Euros* or its equivalent in UK *Pounds* for delivering just a single especially ghoulish or sexually-titillating picture an editor considered sure to boost the sales of his or her cutthroat-competitive British, German, Italian or Spanish lowbrow publication. The paparazzi *looked-like-something-the-cat-dragged-in.* Disheveled, in need of bath, their clothes damp and soiled, they had been camped-out in the square since last night. In order each could maneuver into a physical position to take a "sensational image" of *La Grande Raymonde.*

Television equipment belonging to the *AP, AFP, BBC, Reuters, CNN, NHK* and *Al Jazeera* international news services was being erected to record the coming historic event. "Experts" with slicked-back or dark-roots hair adopted serious, professorial expressions so their audiences at home might believe the commentary they heard was far more knowledgeable than in fact it was. Newspaper reporters scribbled. Atop the mansard roofs of adjacent eighteenth century four and five story buildings stood watchful police sharpshooters. Outside the heavy police barricades a handful of protestors lofted signs in two languages announcing personal opposition to signing a peace treaty.

At sight of the Olympian exiting armored limousine, crowd fell silent.

The hush thundered.

La Duchesse posed for photographers swarming like flies around her authoritarian beauty. The sensual bodily motions she required performing were long ago become instinctive habit. After first, raising two inches further the hem of short, thin, white, silk dress coquettish but dignified; next, projecting ample patrician bust, significant cleavage forward arousing, yet ever-so genteel—the grand lay then, looked imperious directly into the cameras. United with those as captivating as also forever unattainable ladies photographed by Gordon Parks in *Vogue,* La Duchesse delivered with haughty, commanding eyes a message to each of her countless millions of rabid followers across the planet, both male and female. It was a clear unmistakable message:

> *Forget it Joe.*
> *Forget it Josephine.*
> *I'm out-of-your-league!*

"Come closer so you can get an even better picture!" she summoned paparazzi, her melodic voice as flirtatious as disdainful. "Come! You can have some more pictures, some more film of me too."

Snap, snap, snap, snap. Snap, yet more furious camera snaps.

Riveted television and movie cameras hummed.

"Alright gentlemen! If, you actually are *gentlemen*" she abruptly declared. "*Real* gentleman, don't join your—endeavor. La Duchesse won't insult *craft* and *profession* by describing you as possessing one. La Duchesse permitted you taking more than enough pictures and film today. You'll have many more opportunities in near future to again see Madame's legs and bust! Now, off with you cutthroats, *Baccalaureate* examination-failures, transvestites, peeping-toms! Back to your scandal sheets! To your *White Slavery*! Rumor-mongering conspiracies! Now, off-with-you-at-once!"

High Baroque sweep of queenly arm set paparazzi to obedient flight.

"Now shut-up!" whispered Raymonde to Pascale. "Make the crucifix around your neck more visible! Smile humbly; look cute; behave as a *proper* young lady who knows her Bible cover-to-cover. Shut-up! Mistress will plead your case."

"How kind blessing us with your always lovely presence, Rose" exclaimed Cardinal Casimir Blanchard, master of ceremonies. Six-feet-four-inches tall, handsome, powerful, athletic body, he wore a dark, not-off-the-rack three piece suit and conservative silk tie. Only the ring on left hand, medallion around neck indicated he was a cleric.

"I wouldn't miss this event for the world, Your Eminence!" insisted his admirer, barely stopping explosion of teenage giggles. She curtseyed deep, blushing crimson. Next, presented a delicate right hand to be first kissed, then, held. She continued to blush crimson, struggle mightily to prevent explosion of teenage giggles. "When can I expect to read another of your brilliant articles? Did you know I collect them all? At the close of each year I have all those of your fascinating articles appearing in the last twelve months bound? How many annual volumes is it coming to now? I'd rather not say, you, know women are so vain about their age. Anyway, one of the rooms at my estate is becoming a regular *Blanchard Library* or *Blanchard Archive*. Now tell me once more when your next magnificent piece of literature is to appear?"

"On Thursday, Rose" answered Cardinal Blanchard, still holding the lady's delicate hand. "I'm deeply honored at you concluding my scribbling is good enough to be bound. However, I'd wait a bit longer deciding if I'm truly worthy of a library or an archive. You know how much I respect your own erudite opinion, work so hard the quality of my writings always comes up to your own high standards."

"Thursday, Your Eminence?"

"Yes, *Thursday*, Rose. I pray the piece is half-as-good as you hope.'

"Certainly it will be twice as grand as the last, Your Eminence!"

"Have you by chance spoken to Véronique recently, Rose Sweetheart?"

"Yesterday" cooed Raymonde, delicate right hand still in Blanchard's affectionate grasp. "Firebird and I can never survive without our regular weekly girl-chatter on the telephone, Your Eminence."

"Good. Yesterday, by pure accident I discovered a number of personal films I ordered taken but somehow misplaced for a number of years, even forgot existed. One of my 'latest archeological' finds records Véronique's first magnificent performance at the Bolshoi in Moscow. Another records her famous original performance of *Gisele* in New York. In each film, there are three or four occasions where you and I appear seated together in the audience!"

"What can I say, Your Eminence! That's awesome, no, *really* awesome!"

"But that's not all" continued Cardinal Blanchard, warm, protectively. "Finally, I was privileged unearthing a film recording my special Rose at the Frankfurt Olympics winning the Woman's 5,000 and 10,000 meters. Such precious, priceless days gone by! If recalling to Véronique her tragically cut-short career as a prima ballerina isn't too upsetting, I'll be ever-so delighted inviting my two little girls to my residence next month so we special friends can watch the films together, so we can spend an afternoon reminiscing about our soft, splendid memories. Soft, splendid memories I owe to my talented darlings."

"I'll contact Firebird this evening, Your Eminence!" pledged Raymonde, squirming, lovely face crimson. "I know I can persuade Firebird to watch your films. Your two little girls enjoy nothing better than a chance to reunite with our wise, learned, handsome, strong, noble hero. Firebird and I owe everything to Your Eminence's guidance, counsel and love!"

Like Véronique, her closest friend long nourished a desperate *Crush* on Cardinal Blanchard. At Easter time, aged thirteen, home in Paris on spring vacation from the celebrated Normandy convent, Raymonde attended a charity event organized by her parents—the Charpentier clan were for centuries prominent, highly active members of France's practicing-Roman Catholic lay-community. Here, Raymonde was first introduced to the noted-prelate (at the time just Bishop of Tours).

For a nubile convent-girl in *Royal Stuart* tartan, white blouse, monogrammed navy-blue jacket, white bobbysocks, brown, flat buckled-shoes; hair in ponytail; independent contact with males outside relatives and family servants restricted to overweight, balding, unimaginative, fuddy-duddy priests—this chance encounter was unforgettable. Blanchard (then in early thirties), was as charming, engaging, thought-provoking in conversation as later when an internationally-respected poet, essayist. Additionally, Blanchard was as learned as he also eager mentoring the creative aspirations of insecure teenage girls. He was the handsomest, wisest, most intelligent, sophisticated, gifted, appealing male Raymonde ever met.

Two decades and abundant life striving later, nubile convent-girl in Catholic schoolgirl uniform become: La Duchesse owning priceless diamonds, sable coats, style-setting dresses; bobbysocks, replaced with sheerest hose; buckled flat shoes succeeded by heels—Blanchard: now a Cardinal, body no less athletic if hair displaying touches of gray—continued possessing adult-Raymonde's no less passionate, unbounded, near-religious devotion.

Like Véronique, the rare opportunities still obtained to—hold hands with Cardinal Blanchard; to frantically clutch her *Champion*'s arm; to rest her needy, vulnerable, teenage feminine head upon *Cavalier's* powerful shoulder; or, at the upcoming film viewing, be rocked on Cardinal Blanchard's understanding, welcoming lap—were cherished. They, valued infinitely more than far readier, more intimate contact with the President of France.

Wind suddenly blew up Raymonde's short, thin dress.

She screamed.

Lovely body squirming in deepest embarrassment.

Everyone assembled except Cardinal Blanchard, who looked-away, leered.

Raymonde screamed again.

Host of masculine snickers, delighted camera snaps clearly audible.

Raymonde screamed third time.

Only after the wind retreated did she manage keeping the hem down.

"Ah! My dearest Your Eminence" giggled Raynonde flirtatious, pretty face flushed crimson. "Ooh! My own dearest Your Eminence Shame on you! You're not supposed to look up a girl's skirt! Have you no manners?" She was in fact deeply moved Cardinal Blanchard was only one politely looking away.

Two pair of eyes linked long, deep, understanding.

Crowd murmured, reflecting annoyance at the big event not yet begun.

"Hasn't Sister Jeanne arrived, Your Eminence?" inquired Raymonde to master of ceremonies as she closely inspected crowd.

"I've just received a note informing me Sister Jeanne has the grippe."

"*Mercy Me!*" exclaimed the dainty architect of this afternoon's historic event. Her refined heart, lungs and stomach were seized with painful dread. "Is all this work over the many months about to collapse?"

"No, no, Rose!" assured Cardinal Blanchard, stroking admirer's hand, protective. "Sister Jeanne appointed Sister Claire, director of its French branch, to represent their Order at the treaty-signing."

"The Virgin be praised to the farthest creations and beyond!" cried Raymonde with relief. "I thought Your Eminence was about to see a disaster!"

"No fear Rose," promised Cardinal Blanchard. "*Our Lady* is looking well on your noble endeavors. *Our Lady* is looking kindly on the work of all devoted to her. Sister Jeanne will recover in a few days."

"That's good to know, Your Eminence."

Cardinal Blanchard observed silent, humble, four-foot-ten-inch girl at Mme. de Charpentier's side not at all wishing to interrupt her *Betters'* chit-chat. "Who's this respectful darling, Rose?" asked prince of the church. "I don't believe the little Mademoiselle and I have ever met."

"Ah! Yes! Let me introduce Emmanuelle, my most singular lieutenant" informed Raymonde. "I could never survive without Sweetheart at my side. Emmanuelle attends Mass each Sunday, daily throughout *Holy Week,* twice on all major religious holidays. She eagerly performs volunteer work in her parish. Father Castellane's—Véronique's brother—says the child is an immense assistance. Emmanuelle says all her prayers, gives weekly to charity and to a missionary society. She daily recites the *Rosary,* goes regularly to *Confession,* reads the Bible nightly. She always crosses her legs. Emmanuelle never takes the Lord's name-in-vain or associates with unsuitable characters. Loyal, helpful, she can keep a secret. I forbid Emmanuelle to ever wear trousers, watch unchristian-movies or read unchristian-magazines. Such a *Precious, Adorable, Little Thing*, isn't she, Your Eminence? Not another of these

Kittens to-be-had! From instant first setting eyes on *Creature*, I knew I just positively must own her!"

"You're the best, finest acquisition I've made in my entire life, aren't you, *Bunny Rabbit?*" collector complimented favorite doll, stroking treasured her toy's voluminous, shin-length jet-black hair, proprietary. "You're my most prized-possession! An object more valuable than diamonds!"

"In Emmanuelle's birthplace, women still can't vote" Raymonde illuminated. "She doesn't understand politics. I attempted teaching her but politics is hopelessly over the child's sweet, pious head. But like the two of us Your Eminence, she much enjoys following the antics of Sister Jeanne. This afternoon's gathering isn't at all the sort Emmanuelle normally attends. However, since I wanted going to the event with a companion and the child is so eager meeting Sister Jeanne, there was no difficulty persuading her coming along."

She kissed Pascale's forehead, proprietary.

Cardinal Blanchard glanced at his *Louis Vuitton* watch. True to all critical diplomatic summits requiring months of wrangling-negotiations to finally occur, the current one too was opening late.

Raymonde emitted refined artificial sigh. "I deeply regret Sister Jeanne has the grippe. But considering Emmanuelle and I share a mutual interest in the celebrated nun, there'll arise many additional future opportunities for we three ladies meeting."

"I hope this may be only the first time Emmanuelle dear that we cross paths," said Cardinal Blanchard, reaching to paternally shake respectful teenager's hand.

Pascale's four-foot-ten-inch body instantly was seized with physically-painful terror. A *The Creeps* far creepier than any imaginable *The Creeps* propelled by own dynamism, collided swiftly, repeatedly, this-way-and-that, up-and-down, throughout victim's consciousness like a rubber disk in pinball machine gone haywire. Pascale grasped Raymonde's left arm with both own. Limbs clinched, gray-green eyes even when shut swirling in panic, her mouth and throat jammed, heart, lungs raced. Multitudinous jet-black hair descending to shins covered the cute, frightened girl's face.

Blanchard stepped back, startled.

"Emmanuelle's extremely timid, especially frightened of men" apologized Raymonde. Her forced-grin, artificial-jolly, fulsome voice revealed intense personal embarrassment, tremendous annoyance with ward's unladylike-behavior. "Men scare *Pet* absolutely no-end, Your Eminence! Emmanuelle thinks the horrible monsters will gobble-her-up for dinner like *The Big Bad Wolf*! Of course for those responsible for raising girls today, reticence in the *Boy Department* is a blessing! Before placed under my authority, Emmanuelle was an *Army Brat* growing up only on isolated military bases. She's quite unfamiliar with big, noisy cities. Such drastic change over all she experienced before! Still, there's every reason to be confident my *Bunny Rabbit* will in time adjust!"

"Excellent" answered Blanchard, much concerned.

"Normally, Emmanuelle is the gentlest, most deferential, compliant, *Bunny Rabbit* imaginable, Your Eminence" pleaded Raymonde; forced-grin, artificial jolly voice interrupted when wincing in pain from protégée's vice-like clutch on guardian's left arm. "And when Emmanuelle's in her normally obedient frame-of-mind she demonstrates exceptional capabilities. I kid you not! She possesses a truly unique, truly God-given artistic ability! I say so, not simply because Nature designs Mamas physically, mentally prejudiced in favor of their own offspring! No! Your Eminence absolutely *must* see the little creature's magnificent frescoes! The mouse is another Giotto, Fra Angelico, another Goya, Gericault, Rivera! And you must see too the child's splendid lithographs, beautiful sketches! Absolutely superb God-given ability! Emmanuelle is an artist if there ever was or ever will be one! If provided enough adult supervision, sufficient adult encouragement, this child is guaranteed contributing all her immense creative talent to magnifying our faith across the entire world! Emmanuelle's exactly the kind of messenger our faith needs to best represent it during this current alienated, cynical, doubting world!"

"Is that so?"

"I'm attempting to convince *Robin Redbreast* exhibiting the pictures" explained Raymonde, embarrassed. She, dwlivering prophetic glare at gifted but agitated favorite toy. "Perhaps someday soon I can persuade Your Eminence to visit Palais Charpentier and see Emmanuelle's work?

I'll be sure sending the timid-*Precious* on an excursion to my country estate with the other little girls. That way there'll be no repeat of this afternoon's unfortunate episode." Benefactress delivered unruly ward a second angry prophetic glare.

"Is the poor creature going to recover after I leave?"

"Yes, she'll recover, Your Eminence" promised Raymonde chagrined, forcing another wide, embarrassed-grin. "I'm ever-so sorry Emmanuelle's behavior worries you. It's simply that in the part of the world the Dear was born, unmarried girls from *respectable* families have no direct contact with strange men."

"Good, the child will recover. From all you say, Rose, she's a darling *Thing*. I wouldn't want being responsible for making her ill." Cardinal Blanchard made to give a sheltering pat to the girl's right cheek but then knew better. "Hope next we meet you feel better, *Bunny Rabbit*," he said to Pascale. Welcoming expression guaranteeing she was among fellow-spirits.

The crowd shuffled feet in unison, murmured communally louder. Expectation filled air.

The great event was beginning.

"Remember Rose, tell Véronique about the old films I discovered showing my two special girls' triumphs" insisted Cardinal Blanchard. "Please tell Véronique how much I want our threesome watching the films next month at my residence."

"Indeed I certainly will, Your Eminence" responded Raymonde, giggling, deep curtsey, blushing crimson as Cardinal Blanchard again kissed her right hand. "And perhaps when we meet next month I can interest you in coming to see Emmanuelle's superb frescoes and marvelous engravings? You'll definitely admire her work as much as me and Firebird. The child's a little God-inspired artist if there ever was or will be one!"

"Hopefully I can find time" responded departing prelate, noncommittal.

Pascale at last released her protector's arm. She felt terribly ashamed, prayed few others present observed. Thankfully for mortified-*Little Giotto,* the crowd's attention was directed at the event unfolding 50 meters ahead. Girl riveted her gray-green eyes on the centuries' old-cobblestone street, grimaced with pain. Beneath thick, shin-length mane of jet-black hair, tears raised teenage cheeks.

"I've certainly little recommending myself" reflected Pascale, eyes riveted to pavement. "I'm *Just-another-Pretty-Face, Witless Woman.* Destiny needn't fear its throat be grabbed by this Hamlet-in-a-Skirt. I'm so immensely ashamed of humiliating myself in front of Cardinal Blanchard. I see why Mme. de Charpentier so admires His Eminence and wanted His Eminence receiving a good first impression of me. Instead, I behaved like an idiot, caused so much trouble. His Eminence must think I'm just another *Hysterical Female.*"

"Stop at once!" snapped La Duchesse.

"I didn't mean causing a scene, Mistress" replied protégée, sniffling beneath jet-black mane. "I didn' t mean causing—"

"Stop that at once! That's, not how *The Songbird* warbles incomparable melodies! One, who doesn't act beneath herself! Stop that! You won't receive another warning!"

"I'm so-so sorry being a nuisance" entreated Pascale, sniffling beneath vast jet-black mane. Thick, sinuous tresses now completely covered her down to shins. "*Me,* causing a scene after all Mistress's so-kind, so-supportive words, as we were walking over here and in front of your hero Cardinal Blanchard too! And after all my high-minded blabbering! I'm just an idiot! I'm just—"

SMACK

SMACK

SMACK

SMACK

SMACK—on girl's small, tender fanny!

"Any further disobedience, and Mistress will make your fanny as purple as a plumb!"

Pascale was instantly submissive, teary gaze cast at pavement.

Her hands nursing soar bottom, she wept in shamefaced silence.

"Come!" summoned La Duchesse, adopting protective, shielding voice. "Come so Mistress can bring *Robin Redbreast* close."

She took Pascale in own loving, cherishing arms.

Later, after separating girl's thick, sinuous, heavy, jet-black tresses, the Grand Lady kissed fondly companion's wet, penitent cheeks.

Crouching on knees, Mme. de Charpentier warmed contrite protégée suddenly become very cold. "There, there *Pet*! Mistress will make your legs warm again. Cardinal Blanchard's gone now. Mistress takes full responsibility for what occurred. Mistress went about introducing you too swiftly. Cardinal Blanchard can be quite an intimidating figure if never encountered before."

Raymonde wiped *Chere Petite's* teary eyes with silk handkerchief. "Now, here's something you'll enjoy hearing! Every day the other children come to their Mama and speak of how—'Our Emmanuelle makes us feel brave and strong!'—'Our Emmanuelle shows us it's, fun to be—*inquisitive!*' They tell Mama—'We so-love our Emmanuelle for all her constant—*helpfulness.*' They say—'Our Emmanuelle taught us girls can be important, too!' Like Mama they all look up to their Sweetheart. They don't think you're weak or foolish. They know you're strong and bold and daring. And so should you darling! Listen to those who love you my little, un-meddled-with genius and you've nothing in the world to fear! As Christ tells us: *Be, not, Afraid.*"

The animated crowd was abruptly silent.

Eager anticipation filled the air.

"Look!" signaled Raymonde. "Look! The treaty-signing ceremony is about to begin. I brought you with me this afternoon so you might witness a truly historic event, *my* historic event."

"It's only *my* historic event of course" Raymonde insisted "because of the tremendous vision, strength and courage *you* grant me, Emmanuelle! No matter what history books say about *my* diplomacy, I was really just a vessel. This triumph and any others the world chooses crediting me in the future in fact all belong to *you.*"

MESSENGER

....

$\mathcal{F}$or the second time since she "marooned in a land, culture and among a people not my own, rendered forever a stranger," Pascale awoke in the early hours of morning with a fierce, violent start. Just as on that first occasion, this terrifying experience occurred following a month of making very concerted but failed attempt escaping the tenacious, untiring pursuit of troublesome memories.

Two years ago, she was with few interruptions doggedly-chased night and day by the vivid recollection, haunting echo, of Sister Claire gazing enraptured at the New Arena's Chapel's then latest fresco. Pascale was ever-pursued by memory in mind, resonance in ears, of the idealistic young nun sniffling, teary-eyed, proclaiming in stammering, *BBC*-English that Little Giotto was—*The Messenger*.

So too, thirty days were elapsed since the afternoon Pascale humiliated herself on being introduced to Cardinal Casimir Blanchard— renowned-poet, world famous scholar, brilliant art critic and St. Peter at the entrance to France's intellectual paradise. Nagging memory of this incident was for her additionally anxiety-provoking. Not only did touch of any man other than Father give *Chere Petite* a fit of *The Creeps* infinitely creepier than *The Creeps*, it occurring under these particular circumstances, the girl feared, also brought terrible embarrassment to her loving protector and devoted advocate, Mme. de Charpentier.

Just as when two years earlier, mounting anxiety forced open Pascale's gray-green eyes long before she wished, her lungs throbbed, heart raced, teeth chattered. *Goose Bumps* covered *Chere Petite's* jittery arms and legs even if beneath the thick covers she wasn't at all cold. Once again, too, heavy, thick, soupy, blackness enveloped the bedroom, making its shape and dimensions impossible to surmise. She was in the midst of that kind of dark so impenetrable one can walk aimlessly in circles without being in the least aware. Only the sense of touch provided any indication her four-foot-ten lovely-developing feminine body and the mattress it lay upon even existed. Newly open gray-green teenage eyes blessed with perfect vision possessed no better view of the world than ones still closed or even blind.

Pushing massive covering of jet-black locks from pretty face, *Little Giotto* gazed restlessly about. She, at last locating an anemic sliver of ivory-colored moonlight projecting feebly through near all-enveloping, thick, soupy night. This sickly beam constituted the narrow opening between long chintz curtains drawn over a *French window* at foot of oak, canopied, antique bed. Instead of at *La Nouvelle Heloise,* where similar glass panes set in comparable mahogany frame of analogous *French window* opened out upon a townhouse's currently invisible inner quadrangle with gated garden at center paralleled on all four sides by Moorish arcades, beyond the glass at Pascale's bedroom at *Palais de Charpentier* was a rambling, *English Style,* enclosed, private park. At this hour, the impressive grounds accented with an *Augustan Age* artificial lake and neoclassical mausoleum, were all lost in the dark, thick, soupy night.

Nor did the anemic sliver offer any hint if dawn was either just ahead or still many hours to come. If vehicles arriving from central, metropolitan Paris seldom entered the upscale, semi-suburban neighborhood of *La Nouvelle Heloise* even in daytime, no intruders at any hour penetrated the thick, twelve-foot tall, ivy covered red brick enclosing walls of the Charpentier estate. Lack of traffic sound gave no indication as to the current hour.

Pascale's hand steadily groped outward to the right until at last she touching what was in daylight a museum-quality cherry wood *Chippendale* chest of drawers with brass shelf-handles. Hanging immediately above on the papered-wall though also presently unseen in the soupy blackness, were framed color photographs first, of nineteen-year-old Véronique performing *Gisele* at the *Bolshoi* in Leningrad and then of twenty-two-year-old Raymonde atop the awards podium at the *Lisbon Olympics* receiving the gold medal for her first victory at the woman's 10,000 meters. Inquisitive, smallish right hand groping now atop the furniture, "oops," in process knocking a hairbrush on an intricately-woven, ornate and multicolor design *Bukhara* carpet, it finally snatched-hold of a plastic, battery-operated clock whose arms glowed in the dark.

"**3:40**! Goodness gracious me, it won't be light for hours!" groaned Pascale, promptly retreating beneath the covers. She wore a hand-knit nightgown once worn by Véronique. "I usually go to wake up my younger sisters at 7:15. That won't be for hours! And during the night time is so dreadfully slow. It even seems to stands still. Better I try getting more sleep. What does Mama say? 'My growing girl needs to receive the proper amount of rest in order for her to completely develop as she was intended both in as well as body.'"

Pascale's voice was a bit hoarse. It, made croaky as result of all the ecstatic, nearly nonstop-screams she emitted with the rest of the enthusiastic audience two nights ago listening to Matilda deliver another fiery, open-air speech. The notoriety of Pascale's former random flight companion swiftly expanded beyond the confines of the Sorbonne and her National Chamber of Deputies constituency in the 5th Arrondissement of Paris.

From day first elected to an open-seat in the National Chamber of Deputies, Matilda's political star took-off like a rocket. Since its founding through merger of several rival factions at the beginning of the *Twentieth Century*, the Socialist Party of France meticulously avoided promoting one particular class-transcendent domestic issue of often daily concern to all voters. For generations, both the PS's national and local leaders insisted championship or even general association with this frequently burning cultural dilemma was for the Left both ideologically taboo and irrelevant to achieving its historic priorities. Long regarded a "conservative" one, this critical issue was only 'conservative" because the Right took up its advocacy by default.

Since childhood, Matilda believed with the same steadfastness taught by concentration camp-survivor Mama that championship of this "conservative" cause properly belonged to the Left. On being elected, she promptly became first member of the *SP* to champion a "conservative" cause so dear to millions of voters across party lines. Wishing to be in a position to either claim credit for her success or avoid responsibility if she, failed, the *SP* leadership was initially quite willing to let one of its junior elected members chart her own course.

Soon and far earlier than if traditionally embarking on a legislative career as nondescript, unquestioning party backbencher, this particular newcomer emerged as a major, extremely-popular, highly effective if clearly *maverick* spokesperson of the French Left. For hybrid Matilda-Gisela Eisenberg—illegitimate child from a rough neighborhood in St. Clothilde, France; who, made Germany's historic, celebrated Heidelberg glow with pride; a committed *Feminist* so disliking that label; a lapsed-Roman Catholic deeply drawn to the spiritual activism embraced by Jeanne Navarro and her *Sisters of the World;* she, French through place of birth and citizenship but German by surname, mental perception, ethnicity, education and culture; who at university first as student and later as path-breaking researcher gave stodgy, pudgy, conservative academic male hierarchies no alternative to providing her heartfelt respect and admiration—*maverick* was precisely the role suited in the public arena for her immense intellectual gifts. Soon, all the *isms, ians* and *ites* of the Left found they were no better able to control this fierce individualist than the Right had already discovered.

To the inevitable query—"Are you trying to become the secular rival of Sister Jeanne?" Professor Eisenberg always took offense. "Certainly not!" she would reply rigorously. "I simply believe it's a human being's sacred obligation to perform good works, to live a life which *Gives Witness*. To make the world nicer when she dies or at least not worse off than when she arrived in it. I greatly admire Sister Jeanne and the other members of her religious Order but I was above all inspired to take the trail I'm on by a little Sweetheart I met purely by accident on a flight from Frankfurt. I'd mention her name but the darling is terribly shy, bashful. I don't want making the noble soul embarrassed."

73

Pascale was ever-so happy for her friend. "Mme. Matilda is my very first friend, my longest supporter during these years of exile. Mme. Matilda offered me love and companionship before I even knew Mama and Mistress even existed." It was Mme. Matilda who *Little Giotto* first brought within the diameter of her own magic, splendid, personal aura.

"What time is it now?" she asked, reopening gray-green insomniac eyes after indefinite period curled in ball under the covers again asleep. "What time is it now?"

If her heart and lungs returned to normal beat, shivers passed, *Goose Bumps* gone from four-foot-ten-inch body, Pascale continued, save for the sliver of anemic moonlight at foot of bed to be totally enveloped in thick, soupy blackness. The shape and dimensions of her bedroom remained impossible to measure. Both her physical presence and the bed it lay upon detectable only by touch. Once more, she needed to blindly grope with her right hand across the top of the antique, dark-stained, cherry wood chest of drawers with brass handles before seizing the small plastic battery-powered clock with glowing face."4:30! Heavens-to-Betsy! The night will never be over!"

When adolescent feminine eyes reopened at conclusion of second indefinite period curled into ball under covers, glowing face of clock still announced only 4:50.

Girl reluctantly concluded no more sleep was to be accomplished until the following night. After ten additional minutes twisting and turning under the covers to no practical purpose, she once more contemplated the space where in daylight was the room's right papered-wall. On which, though still obscured by heavy, thick, soupy blackness currently hung the framed color photographs of some loved ones. Next to those displaying a prima ballerina and a track star were in pictures of Raymonde's three stepdaughters. Originally brought on to the Charpentier estate to serve as their adolescent nanny/near-age companion, Little Marie's relationship with her charges soon became infinitely deeper, more intimate.

In one picture, Albertine proudly held in each small, resolute hand the brass trophies she just won as winner of both the high-jump and long-jump event during the recent national youth track-and-field meet.

In the next picture, taken at same games, Marie—virgin huntress Diana—already hurled her javelin to victory, now prepared to demonstrate equal prowess at archery. The third image behind the darkness showed the youngest sister, sitting atop "our Emmanuelle's" lap, head cuddled-up to sheltering elder's nicely-expanding bust.

Julienne wasn't old enough yet to prepare bringing the *Charpentier Ladies* still further historic *Olympic* glory. Distance track, pole vault, javelin, long jump, high jump, archery—each, already taken, Pascale considering hammer and discus unfeminine, what gold medal, she wondered remained for baby of the family Mlle. Julienne to seize?

"800 meter hurdles, the triple jump, perhaps?"

Or might possibly Mlle. Julienne demonstrate her clan's athletic skill wasn't restricted to the summer Olympics?

"Why not figure skating? Yes, she will win the gold medal at the winter Olympics at individual ladies' figure skating!"

Our Emmanuelle curled back into a ball. For several fond additional minutes and with strong maternal affection she visualized her third and youngest charge one day executing a matchless brilliant performance before a huge enraptured crowd and host of international television cameras. "The *Mlle. Julienne Maneuver*" imagined young governess, *observing* vividly in mind's eye her third and youngest charge twirling midair six times in nimble succession before returning with utmost elegance to the ice. "No other lady figure skater will ever come near to achieving something as magnificent as the *Mlle. Julienne Maneuver.*"

"In the meantime though, as Mme. de Charpentier—I mean *Mistress*—shows us so well" whispered Pascale at last, "there's more in life, more for a female to achieve than simply fame in sports." Her four-foot-ten-inch body remained neatly coiled in a perfect geometric ball. That same lovely, gentle orb, even if bed covers were pulled off, was totally invisible beneath a vast ocean of thick, heavy, flowing, jet-black tresses. "I must make absolutely sure my three splendid protégées complete all their lessons with no less grace and precision."

Awareness these aspiring little girls were, like their already famous adoptive-mother, given additional worlds beyond *the Olympics* to dominate, couldn't but make *Chere Petite* melancholy.

75

She sighed, shed a tear, sniffled.

"It shouldn't be more than another year until Mistress considers dispensing with my services, or at least those I give Mlle. Marie. If my Mlle. Marie is one day to become the next *Madame La Duchesse de Charpentier* she'll require far more expert, more sophisticated instruction than any I can ever provide. It probably won't be more than another year until my Mlle. Marie is sent to the convent in Normandy."

"It also won't be more than *two* years" added *Big Sister* amid more tears, sniffles, "before my Mlle. Albertine is sent-away to the convent in Normandy, too. I can still hold-on to my Mlle. Julienne five, six or seven years longer but even she'll eventually be taken from me. If Dylan says: *The times, they are a-changing* they aren't a-*changing* as I wish."

She firmly resolved, "I must-must-must-must be sure my girls each complete the lessons I give them with all grace and utmost precision. Do so, if each one is going to be a not just an *Olympic* gold medal winner but a Grand Lady worthy of her Grand Lady mother—"Pascale loyally corrected herself: "I mean worthy of so *great* a great lady as my Mistress, it's imperative in the last months I've got them under me I fulfill my responsibilities."

Those few last words hurled Pascale's thoughts back to the memory of awakening with a fierce start covered in *Goose Bumps*, her heart and lungs racing, teeth chattering.

"Shame on me!" she chided herself. "No! *Double*-shame on me, you *Scatterbrained Female!* More than *Double-s*hame on me! Look how I'm behaving during the last months remaining I'll ever get for having all my girls together! It's my responsibility setting them a proper adult example! It's my duty to be their guide, protector! They look to me to see how adults make proper judgments, rightly conduct themselves! I must do what's rightly expected of me."

"I mustn't do simply what I *want* but what's rightly e*xpected* of me!"repeated Pascale with foreboding. "Women usually don't possess the *Wherewithal,* the intelligence, the emotional strength of character to be entrusted with given responsibility. But, I'm living in the West now. Here, women are given no choice but to try, at least *try.*"

Those words made Speaker cringe in embarrassment. If realizing her lips just spouted a turgid stream of anachronistic, cliché, *Victorian* nonsense, it was impossible for even this most brilliant of women born and raised in a male-dominated cultural to not occasionally be plagued with certain indoctrinated at earliest age self-demeaning fears. Yet as a clear sign these traditions were rapidly losing any significant morbid influence over her decision-making, the girl soon emerged from perfect geometrical ball. Her body shifted on back, arms and legs stretching outward.

Several contemplative minutes elapsed.

Pascale meditated long and deep about her intimate personal relationship with Mama, with Raymonde, Sister Claire, Mme. Matilda and Sister Geneviève. They, and the other adults in Paris, secularist and religious, unfailingly loved, nurtured and protected this brilliant if often tiring to manage little refugee girl. A waif, who three years-ago Fate, or as the victor of the Battle of Heidelberg preferred: Historic Forces Beyond Human Control, abruptly made their unsolicited ward and during the initial twelve months, a near twenty-four-hours-a-day legal, financial obligation.

"Ick!" the small lump on bed commented, mortified, "*twice* ick on me!"

More recently, she, knew, the original, seeming firm-established roles of great benefactress and humble protégée began subtly but in unmistakable fashion, to reverse. *Bunny Rabbit* was steadily the one looked to for nurture, encouragement and protection. Wasn't she becoming lax in fulfillment her new responsibility as the grownups' comforter, guide? Of course, Pascale was, shamefully so. "Double shamefully so!"

The New Arena Chapel was complete. Like the earlier Fourteenth Century sanctuary in Padua, Italy, this second, located in Paris, France belonged not just to a single, unique and gifted creator but the population of the entire world. In addition to constituting an example of enduring, incomparable beauty, a set of 64 near-life-size frescoes remarkable alone for being handiwork of a stateless, teenage girl requiring not a day of formal artistic training to display her genius, her superb achievement presented all lucky enough coming visiting, an essential lesson. One, whose importance transcended all lands, cultures, and, time. The New

Arena Chapel must be appreciated not just among the parishioners of a church in the 5th Arrondissement but admired by all mankind. Once it learned, the lesson Pascale taught the world with plaster and paint would forever benefit each individual woman and man, separate girl and boy across the planet.

8:00 AM declared the small plastic, battery-operated clock, its, arms no longer obliged glowing so their record of passing time be visible. Thick, soupy, blackness once so enveloping it swallowed not just the chamber's size and geometric dimensions but left Pascale only sense of touch to know of her own physical existence, was now fled. The anemic sliver of ivory-colored moonlight feebly quivering through narrow space between chintz curtains was replaced with bold, piercing rays of an ascending sun. Every nick and corner of the bedroom was illuminated. The broad rays created on one section of the bedroom floor a foot long natural kaleidoscope of primary colors—red, blue, green, yellow melding into combinations like violet, orange, magenta and cyan.

The invasion of magnificent natural light gave long-sedentary *Little Giotto* a dynamic, commanding burst of emotional excitement and surge of physical energy.

"We all sympathize, *Sweetheart*" the sunbeams pledged softly, sheltering, maternal. "That's precisely why we've come this morning in such a happy, vibrant multitude. But we didn't arrive simply to offer our sympathy. We've come to make sure our cherished Sweetheart doesn't forget this is the day she firmly takes her place in history! Trust us, darling. Your time is come!"

Pascale scrambled out of her antique, canopied oak bed. She knelt humbly on the thick, sumptuous, multicolored, elaborately-designed, hand-sewn Persian carpet. It was situated atop the center of the bedroom's dark-stained wood panel flooring. Sensuous contours of the girl's four-foot-ten-inch adolescent body were easily delineated beneath a nightgown intended for a woman much taller. She closed eyes, bowed head, clutched, hands in fervent prayer. Following several minutes of silent reflection, she reopened her gray-green eyes, released hands, stood confidently on bare feet.

I am *The Songbird*!" cried Pascale. "I am *The Messenger*!"

BEYOND TIME

The Duchess's long, sleek, shiny, black, feline armored-limousine with clouded, bullet-proof windows; diplomatic license plates; *UN* ensigns floating aloft four corners; possessing for its occupants unhindered communication with all-powers-that-be; motorcycle escort accompanying–sped the Right embankment. The limousine's uniquely-light, highly-maneuverable but extra-thick solid steel chassis and plated-superstructure was both constructed and famously demonstrated ability first: to flip-over three times in a highway collision and settle upright; later, in an assassination attempt: repel four direct hits received from shoulder-fired missiles by Muslim-fanatics seeking to reignite the long bloody civil war only a peace agreement negotiated by a western woman succeeded in ending.

The vehicle performed each deed without its outer walls ever penetrated or windows broken. On both occasions, Mme. de Charpentier came away from the crash suffering only minor bruises, startled heartbeat, shortness of breath, torn hose. Presently, this street-dreadnaught again transported its usual dainty occupants in passenger seat with Ibrahim, 40-cartridge semiautomatic at belt holding the wheel.

"Look, look Mistress, look!" cried Pascale, eagerly gesturing Raymonde take notice. "It's as if a J.M.W. Turner painting! It's as if outside there's a J.M.W. Turner painting in real-life!"

"So indeed, *Bunny Rabbit*, 'it's as if a J.M.W. Turner painting in real-life.'"

"And in Paris too!"

"Yes, *Bunny Rabbit,* a J.M.W. Turner painting in real-life and here in Paris. Now sit still and let Mistress straighten your socks."

High above late-afternoon Paris was a great, awe-inspiring tangerine orb. As it retreated from sight at kingly, no, *queenly*-pace, battlements in the far west changed color from black or sandstone to brilliant gold and auburn. The sky was cobalt blue and lapis-lazuli. As if she providing clear indication that her disappearance was just temporary, the setting sun emitted a final great surge of blinding exuberance. The scattered clouds changed from ivory to scarlet, bright orange and gold. Shimmering silver, beckoning canary yellow, confident indigo and thoughtful russet affected a marvelous watery image across the low far distance. The urban horizon appeared the shore of a broad sea, its natural beauty yet un-meddled with by crude, self-absorbed humanity.

"Like a Turner painting in real-life, Mistress!"

"Yes, Mistress knows" answered she, in a proprietary, otherwise-critically-engaged voice. "'It's 'like a Turner in real-life.' *The Little Sparrow* is ever-so fond of turner. Now, don't move! Child must look *proper* for this special occasion tonight!"

After she first tightening the strap on each of Pascale's high heel shoes, Raymond then lifted her protegée's frock to adjust the girl's panties. That done, the Duchess next, refastened the buttons on the back of the lovely short, sleeveless, red dress she personally selected for her Sidekick to wear this evening. So entitled, confident, was guardian become and her ward cooperative, that the former might seem a dressmaker or department store window exhibit-arranger at work on a mannequin.

"And such a sunset here in Paris, too, Mistress!" reiterated *Chere Petite*, thoroughly engrossed in the spectacle beyond the bullet-proof window. Junior-Rembrandt was long resigned to the Grand Lady believing herself possessing unquestioned-authority to fiddle with mascot's panties, socks and dress whenever whim dictated. She long accepted the peeress's natural privilege to choose Sweetheart's entire wardrobe, selecting each of *Robin Redbreast's* daily outfits. Like an enlisted infantry trooper or able-bodied-seaman commanded by a *spit-and-polish* master-sergeant or an "our branch of the service has the best uniforms"-naval officer, every morning and evening without fail Pascale was summoned for parade ground or fleet maneuvers; her apparel to be meticulously, uncompromising inspected.

"Yes, Emmanuelle, 'such a sunset here in Paris!'" concurred Raymonde, a wide smile on her moist, red painted lips. This expression, represented not so much appreciation of the sunset as satisfaction at altering her understudy's sartorial condition better to own taste. "Most females Mistress had or *has* any extended dealings with aren't up to wearing red. *Red* is very difficult for females to wear and they know it."

Raymonde further dabbled with Little Giotto's panties and dress before resuming counsel. Counsel, she offered to Mini-Velasquez more in the fashion of wise, affectionate, protective, wise sister than as aloof, politically powerful, landed-peeress.

"Most females Mistress has spent significant time with during her sports career, while accompanying Tommy to his government functions, or, when engaged in her own political, social and diplomatic adventures, aren't up to wearing *red*. Not at all! Those making the attempt anyway tend to come-off looking like—lounge-singers, American parvenus, *Kept Women*, lushes, or over-the-hill nymphomaniacs. Worst of all, they aren't even aware how—cheap; 'already-passed-around;' slutty and vulgar they appears!"

"*Red* is the color of colors!" elaborated Raymonde, now adjusting Pascale's collar. The chatelaine's refined, melodic voice confiding, revelatory in tone, mounted in enthusiasm. Intermittently and without noticing, she relinquished addressing protégée in customary *Third Person*. "*Red* is the color of royalty and historic achievement! Of queens, empresses, tsarinas, sultanas, of Sarah Bernhardt, Lily Pons, Geraldine Farrar—red is for cardinals—both with wings and at the Vatican!—*Red* is the color of *Love*—Not of: 'making-love,' or 'did, they make-love?'—as the panderers in Hollywood, on television, on the Internet, in trashy magazines and in those payment-line tabloids make their money persuading malicious dark-roots people to believe! But—*Love. Love* as in *First Corinthians*! *Love* as in Shakespeare's *18th Sonnet* Love! *Love* in the noblest, sense! What did Saint Therese write about that moment when she looked at the sky from the belvedere? Ah yes! *Doubt was no longer possible, faith and hope no longer necessary, love alone made us find on earth Him who we were seeking."*

Out of breath, the Grand Dame fell silent.

While replenishing, calming, her pulsating lungs, rapid heartbeat, she took a hair brush from *Hermes Birkin* handbag. Then, she embarked on the travail of bringing a measure order to Pascale's jet-black, shin–length tresses.

Brush, brush, brush, brush, brush

"Ouch, Mistress!"

Brush, brush, brush, brush, brush

"Ouch, Mistress!

Brush, brush, brush, brush

"The color red is especially a apropos for thwarted love, Emmanuelle" advised La Duchesse. "Never forget red is both the color of Love and that of blood, signifying loss and pain. The love, loss and pain of Pyramus and Thisbe! Remember Thisbe discovers the body of Pyramus dead beneath the red mulberry tree! Mistress speaks of red and thwarted love, not just red and the thwarted, star-crossed love of Pyramus and Thisbe but that too, of Romeo and Juliet—*Death that hath sucked that honey of thy breath, hath had yet no power upon thy beauty. Beauty's ensign yet is crimson in thy lips and in thy cheeks."*

She pecked Pascale's lips and cheeks.

Brush, brush, brush

"Ouch!"

Brush, brush, brush

"The greatest of all Love is the thwarted, star-crossed variety" insisted La Duchesse, hairbrush still valiantly at work. "The greatest of all Love is unattainable or at least not permitted long surviving in this tawdry, materialistic, self-absorbed world. This kind of Love of which I speak is the Love which captures the human heart, forever seizes the human imagination—which inspires deathless art and immortal literature—I apologize for suddenly erupting into this incoherent, rambling, *Scatterbrained Female* monologue. But except for you

Emmanuelle and for Firebird, I possess no one else in the entire world with whom to confide my innermost thoughts and yearnings."

"Fame can be marvelous" elaborated the winner of five gold medals. "Capturing a place is history is in many ways fulfilling. Winning fame and a place in history also set me apart, make me desperately lonely. Increasing, I must exchange understanding-friends for casual-acquaintances. I once possessed His Eminence Cardinal Blanchard to rest my *Witless* head upon, for me to kiss, for me to hold tight, for him to kiss me, hold me tight. His Eminence Cardinal Blanchard was always prepared listening patiently to my *Scatterbrained,* monologues. Time, obligations and responsibilities however make this no longer possible. Today, I've only you and Firebird to kiss and hold tight. I love, adore precious little Delphine, Albertine and Julienne beyond all human description! However, they're each still far too young for their Mama to confide-in. Each little darling is still far too young to understand her Mama's secrets."

Raymonde warmly kissed Pascale clutched her right hand tight.

"This is the greatest of all Love, the Love inspiring timeless art and literature! This form, Emmanuelle, is the greatest union of red and Love—Love and the color red. That is to say—Love—which is either unattainable or not permitted surviving long in this intolerant world."

"Quite an interesting observation, Mistress!" responded her protégée, cognizant of the deeper meaning of words she was just entrusted. "I'm ever sincerely-touched and ever sincerely-honored and ever sincerely-grateful and ever awesomely proud you chose me to make that observation, Mistress."

The girl wanted to say something infinitely more substantial but discovered the proper words to express them suddenly lacking.

"I speak not simply of Pyramus and Thisbe, Romeo and Juliet" continued the Olympian, still holding Pascale close. "I speak of Tristan and Iseult. What did Tristan pledge Iseult and Iseult, Tristan? Ah yes. *Neither fortress, nor tower nor royal prohibition will keep me from the call of my lover whether it be wisdom or folly.* That is Love! I speak too of the love of Abelard and Heloise, of Newland Archer and Countess

83

Olenska, of Feodor Lavretsky and Liza Kalitna, of Jude the Obscure and Sue Bridehead!"

Brush, brush, brush

"Love of this kind is signified by the red rose, the noblest lady in all God's creation! Remember Wordsworth, darling?"

Brush, brush, brush

"*The red rose is a gladsome flower,* Mistress" chirped Pascale. "I never let a day go by that I don't read Wordsworth. Wordsworth is an awesome poet!"

As some others without formal education, *Chere Petite* attempted compensating through becoming a voracious, omnivorous reader. The teenager's bedroom was filled with a mountain of secondhand bookstore-purchased works of great fiction, poetry, biography, philosophy, Darwinism, art history, theology, political theory, astronomy and sociology. Many of the pages of these thick, dog-eared tomes, the pages of frequently reread learned periodicals now often held together only by a paperclip or staple, were heavily marked with the girl's meticulous red ink underlings. Matilda of Heidelberg was well justified in the suspicion her former chance-seating companion on airplane from Frankfurt could later achieve a resounding score on the *Baccalaureate* examination. Owning since earliest age a keen receptiveness to foreign languages, Pascale was completely fluent in six. One, of these tongues being English, she like many artists poetic by nature, Little Giotto required no formal instruction discovering an affinity for "awesome" Wordsworth.

Brush, brush

"*The rainbow comes and goes, and lovely is the rose*" recited Pint size El Greco from Wordsworth's *Intimations of Immortality.*

Brush, brush

"Remember Omar Khayyam?" quizzed Raymonde.

"*I sometimes think that never blows so red the rose as where some dying Caesar bled.*"

"Recall where—*Sweet William on his deathbed lay for love of Barbara Allen?*"

"In Scarlet town where I was born there was a fair maid dwelling"'
responded Pascale giggling a favorite ballad.

"When I was a child at the convent in Normandy" mused
Raymonde, "Sister Madeleine who came—*comes*—from, Britain and
taught—*teaches*—English, also teaches German. She used to sing, still
sings, *Barbara Allen*. She possessed—*possesses*—a wonderful, exquisite
voice. I by-no-stretch-of-the-imagination am sole person believing so!
By no means! Sister Madeleine has a whole repertoire! Besides *Barbara
Allen*, she sings: *La vie en Rose; Je ne regrette Rien; Padam, Padam;
Hymne a l'Amour; Die sieben Todsunden; Die Schone Mullerin; Jezebel;
Mack the Knife; Seerauber Jenny; Winterreise; Ich bin die fesche Lola.*"

Pascale tried visualizing Marlene Dietrich in *Der Blaue Angel*, Lotte
Lenya at a Weimar Berlin cabaret, Piaf on stage at an avant-garde
Montmartre nightclub—each, performing dressed in a nun's habit.

"Sister Madeleine is an exquisite singer!" Raymonde praised her
surrogate-mother. "Mama is a masterful balladeer, a troubadour able to
confront and overcome any other troubadour or silver-tongued cavalier!
And don't think I'm prejudiced in my opinion because of the admiration,
loyalty, affection and trust I hold for Mama—*Sister Madeleine*! The last
time I visited my convent, I finally hounded, whined, badgered, needled,
dogged, hassled, nagged, begged, pestered Mama—*Sister Madeleine*—
long enough to give-in and let her voice be recorded. I provided Mama
with all the finest musical accompaniment, best top-of-the-line Japanese
gadgets, professional staff and space needed to assure the highest quality
recordings!"

Hastily she adding: "I'm by no-stretch-of-the-imagination the
sole person who'll go to the grave sure, absolutely sure that if certain
unexpected events, unforeseen circumstances intervened just to an ever
so-so-so to less degree, if various unavoidable obligations and outside
incidents hadn't managed intruding so strongly at that precise moment,
the world today would speak of Mama—of *Sister Madeleine*—in the
same sentence as Piaf and Lotte Lenya!"

"Awesome! No, it's *really, really, really* awesome, Mistress!"

Raymonde again fiddled with her protégée's socks.

"You know those people haunting Tommy's cocktail parties who claim they attended such-and-such a famous show? Those people claiming they met such-and-such a historic entertainer?"

"Yes I do, Mistress. At church, Mme. Rameau asserts she once dated Yves Montand. I know it's just her fantasy."

Well, Sweetheart, those same people haunting Tommy's cocktail parties would today be claiming to have met or attended a famous show featuring Sister Madeleine! She today would be counted with Piaf and Lotte Lenya! As for Barbra Streisand, Mama is a hundred times better than Barbra Streisand!"

"*Really, really* awesome, Mistress"

"Did you know Sister Madeleine is friends with Bob Dylan?"

"SISTER Madeleine IS FRIENDS WITH BOB DYLAN!"

"No, no, *Robin Redbreast*. It's not what you imagine. Mama was still Miss Beauchamp, then. Also, she and Bob Dylan weren't permitted long enough alone to become eternal soul-mates, spiritually-united companions. There wasn't enough time."

"SISTER MADELEINE IS FRIENDS WITH BOB DYLAN!"

"Once again" lamented Raymonde "larger, unexpected factors beyond both the kids' control intervened."

"SISTER Madeleine IS friends with BOB DYLAN!"

"Mama only got to be alone with Bob Dylan for a weekend. A second opportunity never arose."

"Sister Madeleine was only alone with BOB DYLAN for a weekend! Then other larger, unexpected factors beyond the kids' control intervened" consoled Pascale softly, tenderly. Her teenage brain gyrated with images from *Greek Mythology*; *Gupta Dynasty* statuary; *Nordic Saga*; *Bernini Sculpture* conjecture. "Sister Madeleine was only alone with BOB DYLAN for a weekend. Then never again! It's one of those capricious, malicious accidents of history, Mistress. It's one of those fascinating, eternally-beautiful—*What-Ifs*."

"So it is, *Robin Redbreast*, so it is. Imagine Mama and Bob Dylan! What did Stendhal write? 'It is one of history's–great maybes.'"

"Say, Mistress, when Sister Madeleine and Bob Dylan were alone did they—"

SMACK—on teenager's soft, small fanny.

"Back to our word-game, Child!" ordered Raymonde. "Do you recall what soon was seen between the graves of Sweet William and Barbara Allen?"

"Entwined a love's true knot, the rosebud and green briar"

"And between the graves of Tristan and Iseult?"

"Grew a vine with precious red roses. Signifying their love, if divided in life, is through death united in eternity!"

"Remember Robert Burns?"

"My love is like a red, red rose"

"And when Antony met Cleopatra?" quizzed Raymonde, as if she one of two schoolgirl friends preparing for upcoming British literature examination."

"Cleopatra sprinkled them both with red rose peddles" eagerly responded Pascale as if begging desperately to be called-on by teacher in class. "The red rose peddles were symbolic, prescient too!" Through her voracious independent reading, Pascale had acquired a far deeper knowledge of certain subjects than most receive in school. "Yes, yes, there's the sexual aspect but far more significant is that the red rose peddles warn of future pain and loss. Love, is loss, love is grief, sorrow and abandonment."

The delighted older friend, crossing her legs opposite beneath long gown, briefly set down hairbrush to clap own dainty approval. *"Robin Redbreast* is not only a great artist as the whole world is soon to discover, but a fine scholar!"

Little Giotto blushed.

"And later my *sweetness*, when Cleopatra learned Mark Antony died? The asp she took to bite her breast?"

"Cleopatra took from a collection of beautiful red roses!"

"Also, don't forget the poem by Christina Rossetti?"

"O rose—"

"Miss Rossetti referred to red roses *'so much we need in our weight of woe.'"*

"O rose thou flower of flowers, thou fragrant wonder."

"It appears we're both knowledgeable of literature!" observed Raymonde, giggling like a shielding, big sister, protective older friend chatting with loyal junior sibling, desperately-admiring disciple. As she continued brushing Pascale's jet-black locks her own long coffee-and-cream color hair loosely tied came undone and fell in own charming face.

It seems so, Mistress."

"And who are you to me?" coaxed Raymonde, repositioning a string of natural pearls round young soul-mate's slender neck. "You're, my *Robin **Redbreast**!*"

Next, she opened a makeup kit to repaint Pascale's lips.

"It takes tremendous talent, superb inborn grace for a female to properly wear red, Sweetheart. When wearing red, a female looks either like a queen or a whore! Either a tsarina or one of those American, push-up bra, tramps with dark-roots preying on wealthy old men who ought-to-know-better! Nothing in-between! I've encountered very few females undeniably possessing both the tremendous personal talent and inborn grace to deserve wearing the color of Wordsworth, of Omar Khayyam, of those who die for love of Barbara Allen, of Antony and Cleopatra, Pyramus and Thisbe, Romeo and Juliet, Tristan and Iseult, Abelard and Heloise, Robert Burns, Christina Rossetti. Those few females are: myself; Firebird; Mary Preston, if she only realized her true calling in life; and—you!"

The long, sleek, shiny, black armored-limousine sped the Right embankment.

As brilliant tangerine sunbeams finely illustrated the unique beauty of all below—things: no less small than large; high than low; near and far; in lightness and in shadow—diminished, an onlooker's view of Paris depended increasingly on the assistance of metropolitan, neon glare. Imitation, never the same value as the original, the natural, Turner-panorama changed into a manufactured picture infinitely less enjoyable and stimulating to contemplate. The separate great monuments; divergent wide plazas; broad, sweeping boulevards–each alone, so arresting to behold in daytime, now steadily lost their individuality, independent attraction, following sunset. All but the Eiffel Tower melted into a single beckoning, flirtatious yet thoroughly artificial glow.

"That's a really awesome dress you're wearing. Mistress!" injected Pascale, brimming with teenage-enthusiasm. "You look terrific! When I'm older I hope you grant me permission to wear it. Of course, I'm so short, you'll need getting me a smaller version. I hope when I get to wear *my smaller version* Iappear at least half as splendid as you, Mistress!"

"Thank-you, darling. I do so enjoy wearing this particular dress. I also both pledge obtaining you a smaller version and guarantee you too will look 'really awesome!' Along with me and Firebird, you too are worthy of wearing the color of colors! You too look like a queen!"

Mme. de Charpentier wore a magnificent strapless, backless evening gown; one, rightly befitting her body's natural feminine grace and unaffected ladylike elegance. The vast majority of style-conscious women in Europe, the United States and prosperous, industrialized nations of the Far East like Japan and South Korea could only hope purchasing, marked-down, popular department store, off-the-rack, commercial copies of the majestic clothes in which *Super Models* are photographed and filmed parading the "runway" at prestigious seasonal fashion exhibitions. In stark, genteel contrast, Mme. de Charpentier owned in her immense walk-in closet at No. 4 Rue Marina Tsvetaeva a personal wardrobe restricted entirely to seasonal fashion exhibition "runway," original items. Such luxurious clothing long ago become her daily apparel. She was frequently assumed on the street, in the park, or at Mass by those unfamiliar with her life's story, to be an international *Super Model.*

Such wasn't entirely a misconception. Graceful, beautiful, celebrated; winner of lasting high rare distinction; commanding legions of rabid admirers; compelling in personality as well as body; a-legend-in-her-own-time to most of earth's population–La Duchesse regularly receives and keenly accepts lucrative informal business offers from Europe's most exclusive fashion houses. She on each not infrequent occasion. accepts as much as 15,000 *Euros* along with possession of the suggested garment from top Paris and Milan designers in exchange for appearing at certain nationally-televised cultural, sport or political event wearing a particular new evening gown, cocktail dress, coat, hat or scarf.

La Duchesse is regarded across four continents as the supreme, unchallengeable female-pope of *haute couture.* Top designers naturally agree to pay her vast sums for just a single evening's service, to transforming her huge walk-in closet at No. 4 Rue Marina Tsvetaeva into the ultimate showcase of women's fashion. The initial down-paymentias considered well-worth the expense.

Tonight, escorting Pascale to Little Giotto's televised-introduction to General Public, La Duchesse wore the latest gown created by Milan's leading fashion house. All of her Ingres-physique displayed as if captured in a Gordon Parks photograph for *Vogue* was soft, firm and smooth. Her unblemished skin, was often covered only by impressive yet unpretentious diamonds or discreet touches of an alluring, faraway, vulnerable fragrance.

As on every occasion, the authoritarian loveliness of Mme. de Charpentier's bare shoulders, arms and back was more than just uniquely arresting to visual encounter. Cherished memory of that privileged experience lives on forever dynamic, unfading in both a spectator's heart and in his or her mind's eye. This fondest of reminiscences inspires long and always much-rewarding, fulfilling, meditation.

"You must understand some are coming tonight just 'to-be-seen?'" advised Raymonde of the matchless Shoulders.

"I realize, Mistress."

I

"It would be wonderful if I could get only critics and art historians to see your work, my *Bunny Rabbit*" confided her benefactress. "Unfortunately, that's not how things operate in this cutthroat, Americanized world. Do you understand?"

"I do, Mistress."

"Currently, no one respects an artist until he, **she** is endorsed by the *experts* and permitted into the big galleries. Never mind how brilliant your frescoes, lithographs and drawings are, most people won't appreciate them until the *experts* say to appreciate them or the exclusive galleries ask to display your works. 'If that person is as good as you say, why isn't she praised by the *experts* who know everything or her work hanging on the walls of gallery such-and-such?' It's nice to think talent naturally wins recognition. Sadly, and as I learned well in my own life that's not how the world operates."

"Yes, I do, Mistress"

"Firebird and I aren't thinking only about our Sweetheart's economic security, though of course it's never far from our minds. Since you were stranded in France with almost literally nothing but the clothes on your back you've been dependent even for the roof over your pretty head on charity. Firebird and I haven't precisely made you a scullery maid or forced you to sleep under the basement stairs like Cinderella. But you nevertheless are our total financial and legal retainer. You must eventually achieve the independence that is your due."

"Yes, Mistress, you and Mme. Castellane are concerned about my welfare."

Voice speeding, heart pounding, Raymonde applied Pascale's neck two dabs of her own fetching, pensive fragrance. "Above all else, I'm thinking this evening of *Pet's* long-term reputation as a great artist. I'm thinking this evening of doing all possible *Robin Redbreast's* reputation is spread not only across Paris, France and Europe but across the entire planet. Dying unknown, spitting-up blood in a garret may be fine for an opera. But 'all the world is' not 'a stage.' Nor should it be!"

"This evening Mistress is often overwrought in speech," she confided, after pausing to catch breath. "However nothing can deny *Bunny Rabbit* is more than simply an exceptionally gifted little girl! As yet just a few know the full truth!"

"As yet just a few know the full truth—about what, Mistress?"

Pascale didn't understand what was hinted.

Raymonde made the Sign-of-the-Cross over Pascale's forehead, next, clasped the youngster's hands tight.

"Mistress, Mistress? What's, wrong?"

91

Raymonde waited a few moments to gather her thoughts before kissing Sidekick's hands as one might kiss a Russian icon. When speaking at last, her genteel, melodic voice was with each succeeding word, more reverent.

"Véronique, Sister Claire, Sister Genevieve and I are convinced that you're the new Saint Therese of Lisieux! Not the morbid-sentimentality, touched-up photos, smiley-face, bowdlerized Saint Therese, mind you! Rather, the real, highly-intelligent, authentic heroic girl who wishes to place herself at the table of sinners! The girl who looks after the forgotten, the underestimated, the disillusioned, the lonely and the alienated! Who does so for each and all of them equally! The Saint Therese whose image Piaf always wore as a medallion! The Saint Therese the Mohammedans venerate as a 'Daughter of Allah.'"

Pascale was both incredulous and frightened."

Good Lord!" she thought. "Please no! I've already experienced far more than enough chaos to last several lifetimes. Not this craziness too!"

"Yes, yes, my *Little Flower*" consoled La Duchesse, expecting precisely the reaction her disclosure produced. "At first sight there appeared no similarity between you two kids, I readily admit. You and Saint Therese come from such diverse time periods and social, economic, historical, geographic backgrounds."

"In addition" she continued, "while Saint Therese only once left her native Normandy and became a cloistered Carmelite nun, you, *Bunny Rabbit* are from the Middle East, now live in a metropolis, are familiar with all sorts of cultures and want to be a famous painter! Also, whereas Saint Therese died in total obscurity, her greatness only recognized by the world after her death, my *Robin Redbreast* is sure being recognized in her own time! Save for a common deep faith, common high intelligence, there's no resemblance between you kids."

"No similarity between you two girls occurred to me" she admitted, "until certain characteristics were brought to my attention in recent months. Afterward, I was dumbstruck, taken-aback, almost physically overwhelmed at not long ago immediately identifying the so obvious, so clear, so apparent-to-the-eye similarity between you two noble, precious, heroic kids!"

"You girls" pledged Raymonde, "are spiritual twins with twin souls, twin hearts and a single message! 'of us" teaches you two girls *Little Way*, even the least of us, can equally honor and serve and love and do justice to God! Can equally be one with Christ and Christ with us through dedicating our lives to Him in our own personal, earnest fashion! We don't need to be princes and theologians, *experts* or *authorities.*"

Pascale felt a sudden desire to run away.

Took step to flee.

"You teach the same exact message as Saint Therese!" insisted Raymonde in rambling deadly earnest, meandering absolute conviction.

She, promptly seized firm grip on her companion's hands to prevent flight.

"The only difference is that your social, cultural, political background, life story, are adjusted to better suit Saint Therese's message in today's society! Humanity has grown far too materialist, secular, defeatist, self-absorbed to ever follow a Carmelite nun. Luckily, providentially, my Sweetheart's been chosen to assume this role. Here in the West as well as in Asia and Africa! No less than it did once St. Therese, the contemporary world will now gladly listen to, eagerly follow *Robin Redbreast!*"

"Véronique, Sister Claire, Sister Genevieve and I" pledged Raymonde, "all sincerely believe you're the new Saint Therese! She delivered her message in a priceless book. But since today so many people no longer read or appreciate books, even know books should be read, appreciated—you deliver your message through frescoes and lithographs! Just as the deceptively-simple, deceptively-commonplace account in *Story of a Soul* immediately captured the imagination of hundreds of millions across the planet, so too, now, your own deceptively-simple and seeming-amateur, as approachable as brilliant style of art, will capture the imagination of our century!"

Pascale squirmed but Raymonde wouldn't let her go.

"Don't be frightened *Pet*. I know what you're thinking—'People will laugh, will sneer at us, will dismiss us as 'barefoot, backwoods, *Scatterbrained Female* provincials!'—But no one can possibly accuse Firebird, Sister Claire or Sister Genevieve of being troglodytes or *Witless*

Women! Firebird, who still might be the world's *Prima Ballerina Absoluta*, isn't precisely an illiterate peasant with no teeth and fifteen children! Or an obscurantist, superstitious crone who's, never seen a light-bulb, a railroad or traveled twenty miles from the place of her birth!"

"Sister Claire and Sister Genevieve aren't exactly traditional nuns" illustrated Raymonde."Nor are they looked upon with favor by the conservative all-male hierarchy in Rome! No one ever accused their Order of raising money for Franco; of saying: *We didn't know;* or sheltering Collaborators!"

"Sister Claire, Sister Genevieve, Véronique and Mistress" assured the latter, "all of us become still more convinced of your true identity, each time we look at the walls of the nursery school and of the New Arena Chapel!"

"What does Father Richard say?" interrupted Pascale stammering, finally pulling hands free, attractive teenage body cringing with anxiety. "What was the reaction of Father Richard? Since Mama is his blood-sister I assume she told him her opinion."

"Father Richard's a physician, a scientist. Father Richard was educated to be suspicious! He's an archeologist too. So he naturally wishes making decisions based on evidence he can touch. He told Firebird—'Hush-up such talk or our parish will be overrun with scandal-sheet scribblers, Latin Mass-reactionaries and American *New Agers*.'"

"Of course" commented Raymonde knowingly, "Father Richard also wears trousers! He's far less-perceptive than we who wear skirts!"

"*Me*: a saint?" stammered Pascale. "*Me*: a Saint Therese?—Mama believes it and—you too Mistress!—Sister Claire, Sister Genevieve, also? I—*me*—what've I said or done—or how've I conducted myself so you and Mama oand the Sisters—I'm so sorry I've ever done or behaved in a way that I led you to believe--"

Additional words failing, she broke into tears.

"Precious! exclaimed Raymonde with delight, "you *Piaf-not-on-morphine*! You're too simple, innocent, uncomplicated to realize your own exceptional value! I expected this self-effacing, pious, modest reaction!"

La Duchesse kissed *Robin Redbreast* on right cheek.

"It's only what I expected! It's only what's proper to assume from a dear of your remarkable kind!"

Pascale's vehement, confused, garbled attempt at denying sainthood served to just strengthen her advocate's conviction. "Tomorrow, I must write to Mama—*Sister Madeleine.* Sister Madeleine and the other nuns at the convent will certainly wish meeting you, Sweetheart."

"Father Richard commanded you to *hush-up*!"

"Yes, yes. I'll obey Father Richard at Mass!" assured Raymonde. "I also won't tell Sister Madeleine to inform Bob Dylan yet!"

"Sister Madeleine won't tell Bob Dylan yet!" Pascale sighed with relief.

"Sister Madeleine likely will reprimand me for even mentioning this news outside church" predicted Raymonde. "But since I was a child I keep Mama regularly informed of all I do. Remember, she's the one ultimately responsible for my five gold medals at the *Olympics*. Mama can be depended upon to keep this news *hushed-up* until Father Richard can be prevailed upon to change his mind. Mama won't tell Bob Dylan yet."

The great, fiery tangerine orb had completely descended below the distant west. The sky above metropolitan Paris was uniformly black. The long, sleek, shiny armored limousine now sped an embankment visible only with the aid of vehicle headlamps and garish, sometimes blinding streetlights.

All the distinctive sites of Paris save the *Eiffel Tower* were unrecognizable except at relative close distance. Each, save the *Eiffel Tower* became enveloped until the following dawn in thick, soupy darkness. A darkness, even the brightest neon glow could just partially, intermittent and briefly penetrate. At this hour, view from a car racing the embankment was generally little different from that available to motorists hurrying the highway of any major city intersected by a river.

"In order to get the international press to report on your New Arena Chapel" explained Raymonde unperturbed by protégée's efforts denying special status, Mistress needed creating all the frantic, lemmings-off-the-cliff hoopla in *Figaro* and *La Croix* and on the airwaves you've read, heard and seen during the last month. It's not pretty but in this economy the tactic is necessary. Remember too all the pandering, cloak-and-dagger, Florentine, back-door maneuvers that were connected to finally publishing *Story of a Soul*!"

Beneath vast jet-black tresses, Pascale again grimaced. She closed gray-green eyes tight. Once more attempting but failing to release her hands from Raymonde's impassioned grip, she clinched each in a rigid little fist. The discovery that her protectors—two of them nuns—believed she was a saint made Pascale not merely embarrassed but ashamed.

"I've received more than a few bouquets prior to your arrival on the scene, Divine Child" mused Raymonde. Tears of happiness ran her brown eyes as she removed an elegant handkerchief from *Hermes Birkin* handbag to wipe Pascale's unblemished cheeks. "At the Frankfurt Olympics, I received a fabulous bouquet of red roses presented to me by none other than Emil Zatopek himself! I received a wonderful bouquet each time Tommy was elected president, others at the summits I accompanied Tommy. I received beautiful flowers upon my appointment at the *United Nations* and at the signing ceremony for the peace treaty I negotiated."

She cast Pascale a glance of infinite longing.

"But never in my wildest dreams did I imagine being given—*The Little Flower*!"

II

Snap, snap, snap, snap, camera snap

The long, sleek, shiny, black armored limousine was instantly engulfed in mob of thrilled, excited *AP, BBC, AFP, Reuters, CNN, NHK, Al Jazeera* print and wire-service reporters. The vehicle slowly navigated a stormy ocean of international cable television and radio teams, making its way passed swarming paparazzi catering to mass-circulation Right-wing French, British, German, Italian and Spanish tabloids; each photographer frantically crackling Japanese gadget.

Such frantic, congested-humanity assembled in the narrow, serpentine, cobblestone streets of the Left Bank's *Latin Quarter*, a car built to withstand shoulder-fired missiles could only advance at human's slow walking pace. Finally, Ibrahim, 40 bullet-clip semiautomatic at belt, parked adjacent to front portico of the nine-hundred-and-fifty-year-old Romanesque/Gothic church of polymath-Richard Castellane. If the physical location is easily missed by those unfamiliar with the *Latin Quarter*, the structure's leaping spires make its presence in daylight, boldly apparent far away.

Snap, snap, snap, snap, snap, snap

Within these granite medieval walls, one of the most remarkable exiles ever settling in Paris began her historic career. When Pascale Kedari/Marie Castellane first arrived three years earlier, no one but a handful appreciated the virgin's talent or expected it to prosper. "The illegal alien child's work is—*interesting*;" "the Muslim girl's pictures are—*different*" pronounced Mme. Rameau, expressing judgment not simply of the church office biddies but of the vast majority of parishioners taking any time to look at the *projects* which *goodhearted, charitable*-Father Richard *permitted* "his sister's *maid* to *indulge*. Even the suggestion this waif might wish redecorating the chipped, peeling, plaster walls of an unused, side sanctuary was originally offered simply as means to distract her from homesickness, suicidal thoughts. No one, not even the artist herself expected this *project* to become the New Arena Chapel.

For Pascale, this evening's event should have been the happiest moment of her life, climax of a career the Divine Child had in fact barely begun. Instead, *Chere Petite's* mind was desperately troubled.

"Here we are at last my darling, precious Beloved One!" exclaimed Raymonde amidst frantic tears, of joy. With immense reverence, desperate humility, gestures often interrupted by joyous emotion, she made the *Sign of the Cross* over Pascale's forehead. "The moment has come my own Saint Therese! My darling, precious saint! It's time, the whole world discovers the fabulous mission only a few other little girls were ever privileged by Christ to fulfill!"

"Here is your moment!"repeated La Duchesse, amidst sobs of boundless elation. "Here's your moment! Show me the way Beloved One! Show me the path, Therese! We'll begin tomorrow at first light. Or as Bob Dylan would say—*In that jingle, jangle morning, I'll keep following you.*"

She embraced Pascale, showered the girl's face with heartfelt kisses. "Lead me Beloved One!—*Take, me far passed the twisted reach of crazy sorrow.*"

END PART ONE

FAME

....

ittle Marie's fresco commemorating the historic Middle Eastern peace treaty negotiated by Raymonde de Charpentier is her finest creative achievement to date. If our magazine in the past was less enthusiastic about Little Marie's work it was simply because negligent city fathers failed providing the unique teenager sufficient space and opportunity to fully express her immense artistic talent. Finally, this naturalized-French citizen can exhibit our own institution's ideals at their purest. As our institution's best modern advocate, ablest contemporary representative of its principles, we give Little Marie our warmest, most heartfelt salute—"

"Oh, blah and yet additional sycophantic, obsequious bloody waste of ink blah, blah!" summarized Sister Claire, cutting-short her perusal of the nation's most famous and influential art magazine. It was a monthly journal long recognized throughout Europe as the unofficial mouthpiece of the French intellectual *status quo*. "I've seen this same kind of 'quick-get-on-the-ferry-before-it-leaves-us-behind stranded' jabber from these bigoted fools too often before!"

The nun delivered the same curt judgment as might an overworked secondary school teacher. One, compelled to plow-through dozens of slapdash, repetitious, mediocre entries to a regional youth essay contest.

A sudden, exceptionally loud groan by tugboat cruising the murky Seine, appeared to register the vessel's firm, chivalric sympathy.

"Oh, blah and additional sycophantic, obsequious, bloody drivel" reiterated the pretty social activist, fiery-red hair beneath her veil. She,

99

offered the tugboat a warm smile of appreciation. "The reactionaries are trying to take credit for my Sweetheart's genius, to assert they fathered my Divine Child's mastery! Of course, who was it, Joseph Addison, maybe? Yes, it was Joseph Addison who said: 'Imitation is the sincerest form of flattery.' I presume the world doesn't truly recognize the value of an individual's accomplishments until the world tries stealing credit." Fiery-redhead paused. "It's bloody *common*! It's so bloody *common*!"

Sister Claire was now headquartered in Paris for ten years. So busy was she taking responsibility for all members of her sisterhood in France, Belgium, the Netherlands and Luxemburg, this nun could converse, read, deliver lectures or speeches in French, German and Dutch so fluently, each was often mistaken as her native language. Yet whenever alone or among close friends, the erstwhile-duchess invariably reverted seamless to her childhood and adolescence's *BBC*-English. Presently, it was a slightly off-color *BBC*-English.

"Enough of that *Grub Street* hack-journalism!" insisted the former-Lady Mary Preston, she no less capable of *High Baroque* gestures as Mme. de Charpentier.

She hurled the prestigious bimonthly into a steel trash bin, at side. *Plop*!

Following a meandering stroll through the center of the French capital, the chief lieutenant of Sister Jeanne Navarro rested atop a wooden bench. It was situated within the twenty-acre Place de la Concorde adjacent the neoclassical Fountain of Commerce. In one direction was observed the Pont Alexandre III, the Musée d'Orsay, Les Invalides, Palais Bourbon, the Eiffel Tower. From another, could be seen: the Luxor Obelisk, Hotel Crillon, the Rue Royale and the Madeleine. Visible from third direction were the Tuilleries Gardens and the Louvre. Seen from yet fourth angle were the Champs Elysée and Arc de Triomphe.

If she was known collectively to MI6, the CIA, KGB, French, Chinese, Saudi foreign intelligence services and Interpol as *The Red Virgin*, her name for a decade appearing on the McCarran-Walter Act list of "subversive aliens" denied visa to United States–this renegade-aristocrat was also ever-meticulous sitting upright, her charming lower limbs crossed. As her governess Mrs. Anderson taught—"A *proper* British lady of ancient family who was presented to the Queen doesn't slouch or fail crossing her legs!" If later traveling a different path than other girls in her rarefied, landed-elite, even cynical Paris police readily-admitted "Sister Claire is always a *proper* British lady wearing a *proper* dress or *proper* skirt."

Her reputation created no obstacles to she winning extensive trust and support among communities far less economically privileged. Had the 23rd Duchess of Airandel just been *Slumming-it*, only *Curious-to-see-how-the-other-half-lives*, simply *Going-through-a-phase*—concluded longshoremen, factory employees, agricultural workers and trade union organizers, *Milady* would have long since tired "meeting the peasants" and retreated to comfort of her own wealthy, titled, land-holding origins. As was soon apparent to all encountering her, Uncle and Auntie's adventurous niece was made of sterner intellectual, spiritual, if not bodily stuff. Although never once diminishing the clearly patrician flavor of her personality, Sister Claire eagerly embraced what she considered her *Vocation* as champion of the downtrodden. Sister Genevieve Fauré was only the first of many in the European working class wishing to serve as this noble-hearted but physically-vulnerable upper class girl's confidante, guide and protector.

Sister Claire next perused the journal of the French creative *avant-garde*.

"Tuesday marks the opening of the newest art exhibition of Little Marie Castellane. So furious was competition between prestigious galleries to host the event, only yesterday it appeared the show might be either canceled or postponed indefinitely. Thankfully, just hours ago attorneys for rival parties reached final settlement on selecting a neutral venue. Due to intense demand for tickets, length of the retrospective is extended two weeks. The tyranny of outmoded concepts is at last dead! With the phenomenal works shown in her latest exhibition, Little Marie forever sweeps aside the rigid traditionalism continuing to blight so much our city. This young artist is exactly what our cause needs at this crucial moment in western culture. As our most outstanding champion and disciple, we look forward to her many years of success—"

"Oh yet further blah, try-to-steal-the-credit, blah!" abruptly concluded Sister Claire in *BBC* English, promptly enabling both magazines share company in trash bin.

Plop!

"Sweetheart, priceless darling, before all the *experts* and *authorities* recognized your magnificent talent, I saw it, knew it first!" The nun experienced the immense joy, surging rightful-pride of a Mama observing world finally recognize the brilliance she knew her child possessed from moment giving offspring birth.

As was become her alternative-religious habit, Sister Claire wore a light-gray woman's business suit with skirt hem above knees; white, frilly-blouse, black ribbon at neck; sheer hose; black heels; wide chapeau atop extensive screaming-red hair. A big leather bag with long strap was suspended from her jacket's left shoulder. Only wa ooden crucifix at bust attached to necklace and metal band on left ring finger indicated she was a Roman Catholic religious not an attorney, university professor, or other successful and ambitious woman in secular society.

"Heavens-to-Betsy! I'm late!" the nun cried, glancing at watch. "I'm dreadfully-late!" Rising to feet, she scampered-off as fast as high heels permitted.

During the past nine months, Sister Claire and Sister Genevieve were no longer privileged being Pascale's near-inseparable copmpanions. The many commissions Little Giotto now received to paint public murals and church frescoes compelled this once tight-knit trio mistaken for siblings to be often apart. Véronique still enabled the friends to link-up each Sunday for Mass at Father Richard's church in the 5th Arrondissement and at holiday dinners at *La Nouvelle Heloise*. Yet these formal occasions were never as emotionally-fulfilling as opportunities for private *Girl-Talk*. This particular afternoon was one of the rare chances offered for a more intimate encounter. Sister Genevieve certainly would have come too. However, she was dispatched on an assignment for her social-activist Order, abroad.

I

"What first motivated you painting, Little Marie?" shouted a print journalist, he struggling o be heard above the roar of wind and traffic.

Newspaper photographers snapped away their Japanese gadgets. Members of the *AP*, *AFP*, *Reuters* and the *BBC* narrated the ceremony into hand-held phones. Television cameras rolled.

"When I was a kid, Father gave me a book containing photographs of famous paintings!" replied Pascale, endeavoring to be heard above traffic roar. She held her Edwardian chapeau with both hands in order to prevent the huge headgear from flying off to who-knows-where. "The photographs were awesome! Like all girls I love pretty things! So, one day I thought it might be fun making a picture myself! One thing led to another and so here I'm speaking with you this afternoon. I guess I must have a small degree of talent because I've been at picture-making ever since! You and the city government seem to agree!"

Following her completion of a mural celebrating the peace treaty negotiated by Duchess Charpentier, *Chere Petite* was commissioned to paint another panorama above the front entrance to a major public building. Unlike the earlier work, located in a generally-quiet and secluded urban square, this later masterpiece is found running part of the Right embankment. On today's occasion, the steady-roar of vehicles speeding an adjacent highway paralleling the Seine along with strong gusts of wind combined making it especially hard for the voices of pedestrians to be heard.

"Little Marie, are you The New Europe?" inquired another news-gatherer.

"*Me*? Goodness-gracious!" answered Junior-Rembrandt demure, her hands still guarding huge headgear, shin-length ocean of jet-black hair flapping in wind. During the last nine months, *Chere Petite* learned to detect press questions designed to solicit controversial political statements, provoke newsworthy gaffes. She also learned how to effectively parrying them with polite, noncommittal-replies. "Last week a journalist asked if I'd become the New Something-else-or-other!"

"Little Marie, as a practicing Roman Catholic and friend of the clergy" baited the next scribbler eager for a headline, "please provide us insight into the recent comment by Pope Francis on the domestic policy of President Belanger?"

"The Holy Father's perfectly able speaking for himself, Monsieur."

"Little Marie, we know your financial-backer is Cardinal Blanchard. Is the Cardinal soon going to directly enter electoral politics?"

"I receive no financial-backing from Cardinal Blanchard! In addition, as a member of the clergy, His Eminence isn't permitted *nor* is he *desirous* of holding secular office!"

"Little Marie, you often use mixed-colors like orange—a combination of red and white," asked reporter with dogmatic tone of speech. "Does your latest work declare contemporary political and social strife in Europe can only be solved through racial intermarriage?"

"You've made a singular interpretation!"

"Is this mural your testament, Little Marie?"

"It's a piece of *art*, Monsieur."

"What is its *meaning*?"

"I leave that to viewers."

"Little Marie? Do you scorn *convention*?"

"I paint, Monsieur."

"Are you a *rebel*?"

"I'm sure you've already made up your mind!"

"Little Marie, are you *The New Woman*?"

"I just painted the *new* fresco."

Regular newspaper photographers and independent paparazzi catering to celebrity-oriented tabloids furiously snapped Japanese gadgets.

Television cameras belonging to *CNN, BBC* and *France 24,* hummed.

Members of local and national radio services brought microphones nearer.

"Some claim, Little Marie, your new fresco advocates redrawing the political boundaries of the Middle East" returned the dogmatist. "Some claim this new fresco announces your solidarity with the struggle to combat United States imperialism? Do you endorse economic sanctions on Israel? Are you calling for Israeli leaders to be brought before the World Court for committing Crimes Against Humanity?"

"I neither now nor in the past ever expressed or harbored any quarrel with Jews or the state of Israel!"

"Little Marie, when, are you converting to Islam?"

A further strong wind arrived off the murky Seine.

Pascale screamed.

An amused male audience carefully followed the teenager's predicament.

Pascale screamed again.

Additional newspaper and magazine photographers eagerly took pictures.

Snap, snap, snap, camera snap

Pascale screamed third time.

Snap, snap, snap camera snap

Hers was a dilemma long, arduous, if for spectators, ever-memorable.

"What a nice little fanny!"

"Exactly appropriate for those terrific legs!"

Pascale screamed yet a fourth time.

At last, fighting heroically, the poor girl regained control of situation. "Am I converting to Islam?" she giggled, hair over face, hands desperately grasping swift-flapping miniskirt. "Would I confront these—episodes—if I were converting to Islam?"

Then, just as Mme. de Charpentier taught when she caught in a similar embarrassing predicament, her Sidekick instantly blushed crimson, whimpered vulnerable. Next, she provided male spectators a flirtatious wink, rewarded viewers with a knowing, coquettish feminine smile.

Much additional amused middle-aged masculine commentary passed among the delighted crowd.

"Do you support giving resident non-citizens the right to vote in municipal and regional elections, Little Marie?" the dogmatist renewed. True to calling, nothing distracted him from original goal.

Interviewee in short skirt contemplated following move

She batted painted eyelashes, smiled, demurely.

"A simple, uneducated, provincial creature like me is the last person on earth one should ask for advice on politics!"

She giggled

Breeze at last subsided, Pascale judged it safe releasing hem.

Audience murmured disappointed.

Other reporters previously unheard, swiftly raised hands seeking recognition.   "Little Marie!"

"Little Marie!

"Very well gentlemen" *Chere Petite* declared monarchical. "If you characters really are *gentlemen*!" Recent personal embarrassment in instant vanished, arms energetically akimbo, her lively gray-green eyes projected triumphant authority. "Didn't we assemble this afternoon to talk about my recent public commission for the plaza?"

Robin Redbreast dearly hoped Mistress would be watching her *Pet's* interview on the evening's television news. "Let me simply start-off" said *Cherie*, "by saying I'm ever-so awesomely honored to be selected by Duchess Charpentier and the neighborhood fund to carry-out this project. I'm awesomely honored, especially as the first girl, the first *lady* entrusted with fulfilling such an awesome project. I hope my work meets Duchess Charpentier and the fund's specifications and also hopefully, provides passersby a bit of pleasure. Considering where I was only a few years ago, it's still hard believing what's happened since! I'm sure the press is curious learning how the project came to be and how Duchess Charpentier chose *me* as its creator. I'll be delighted answering all serious and legitimate questions in detail and at length. Please feel free to ask me. I hope I can transfer a measure of the excitement this awesome event gives me personally to the larger, General Public."

"Please! Speak up!" she cried. "I'll be delighted answering all your serious and legitimate questions in detail and at-length. Come, you rascals! Speak up! Or should I conclude Frenchmen are scared of girls?"

Bunny Rabbit's outstretched arm and forefinger swept her submissive male audience in majestic challenge, left-to-right. "Mistress will be proud of me" thought *Pet*. "Of course I'll never be as good at handling people with trousers, as can Mistress. Mistress is after all, well—*Mistress*. She dwells in a higher dimension!"

"Please!" *Bunny Rabbit's* commanded the journalists awed to silence by this Divine Child's instinctive grandeur. "Ask me a serious question about my fresco."

"Little Marie is most grateful for your attention" announced Sister Claire as the nun suddenly emerged from crowd. "Unfortunately, Sweetheart needs to leave now!"

After directing the last questioner among the press an especially nasty glance, Sister Claire took young friend firmly by left arm and whisked her away.

II

"Please forgive me?" begged Sister Claire as the soul-mates meandered a quiet, ivory-gray, residential side street. Bronze historical markers were placed above several front doors. "I'm so terribly sorry not arriving earlier! A *proper* young lady like you shouldn't be without a chaperon when faced by a cohort of dim-whit, randy middle-aged men! I promise never letting this happen again! Never! My mind was wandering. I totally forgot the time! Please forgive me? And please don't tell Leopoldine or Mme. Castellane about my negligence? I swear never again leaving you unchaperoned!"

"Don't be upset, Sister Claire" insisted Pascale soothingly. "I know only the most urgent matters were holding you up. Anyway, I never doubted for an instant you'd eventually come and rescue me!"

STe girl rose on tiptoes to give her anxious protector a kiss on right cheek.

Sister Claire felt very stupid.

"Please don't talk to me *like that*, darling!" she implored. "I don't want you ever thinking you've got to talk to me *like that*! I understand that in the months since people discovered the New Arena Chapel you've learned how to manage crowds. You've learned how to negotiate the world without my constant chaperoning. Please forgive me!"

"How do you mean, Sister Claire?" answered Pascale, pretending not to understand.

"If I ever interfered in in the past—"

"—it's only because you love me!"

The two girls walked for several minutes in silence, hand-in-hand. It was a tender, engaging, comradely silence ever cherished.

"How do you like my new heels, Sister Claire?" asked Pascale at last, raising one foot, then the other. "All my life I dreamed of having ones this color! Passing them in a shop I just couldn't resist! After all, what's life worth without *these* heels?"

"I can't imagine"

The pair crossed a stone bridge from the Right embankment to the Ile St. Louis. What a change! Just a few hundred meters away, the modern city and its self-absorbed multitudes thundered on speedy, impersonal journey. Here, on this smaller island in the middle of theSeine, the girls rambled quiet narrow, cobblestone streets through sleepy, thought-provoking, ancient neighborhoods. Yet even this sanctuary wasn'tt immune to sorrow.

"Do you remember any sad epitaphs?" inquired Sister Claire.

"Here lies a man whose name was writ in water'—John Keats."

"Yes, that one always gets me, too! However, it's also so romantic. And we both know the name John Keats is now 'writ'—in stone."

Theduor stopped outside the old, mansard-roofed residential building at No. 19 Quai Bourbon once inhabited by Camille Claudel She, at last recognized by the world as a great sculptor. An acknowledgment her manic depression, mother's bitter jealousy and sexist *Napoleonic Code* reducing women to disposable family chattel prevented achievement during lifetime. A particularly grim, highly ungenerous historic marker was engraved above the building's front door. Here, in a street-level studio Camille Claudel worked prior to being imprisoned at her mother's request and brother Paul's compliance for the rest of here long life in an insane asylum.

"This *one,* though" observed Sister Claire, gesturing to plaque "is as dreadful as you're ever going to get."

"Is that so?"

"'*Here: Camille Claudel—sculptress:* "*lived and worked on the ground floor and courtyard from 1899-1913. It was on that later date her brief career as an artist ended and she commenced her long dark night of pain and confinement.*'"

"Ooh!"

"And look, Dear!" indicated the nun, again gesturing to plaque. "There's also this quote underneath from a letter Camille wrote to Rodin: '*I've always possessed an inner-torment*'"

"Icky! *Double* icky! *Triple* Icky!"

"And look! The plaque was placed there by her brother! He effectively writes-off everything his sister ever accomplished! He makes poor Camille a faceless nobody. What does it make me think of? Remember Bob Dylan?—"*With no direction home/Like a complete unknown/Like a rolling stone*"

"Her brother was largely successful" commented Pascale. "None of the art books I had where I was born contain any reference to Camille Claudel. Personally, I think her brother was jealous!" Then, upon adjusting chapeau, Pascal observed, "In those days it didn't pay for girls to have brains!"

"I've always possessed a particular affection for Camille" revealed Sister Claire. "One day, you might create her a more fitting memorial."

Pascale meditated again, adjusting skirt "Why wait for me? Why don't you do it, Sister Claire?"

"Who, *me*," was reply, dubious.

"Yes, by all means, Sister Claire! You're the writer! You're the one knowing Camille's story!" encouraged Pascale, rising on tiptoes to kiss her friend's left cheek.

A gust of wind blew in.

This current made more furious by traveling serpentine streets.

"Oh!" Pascale cried. "See what's just been done to my hair! It's been blown every-which-way! It's all tied-up–in-knots! I can't go home like this! Mme. Castellane and Duchess Charpentier will think I've been up to something not *proper!*"

The girl frantically searched purse for hairbrush, eyes tearing, voice breaking.

As much as she wishing to assist her little friend, observation of the child-genius's plight created in Sister Claire's mind a sensation of deepest tenderness. An unrivaled tenderness for a moment Sister Claire prayed might never cease.

"Come on!" she instructed after the longest few seconds in life. "It's still too windy for you to manage on the street. I live not far away on the West Bank. You'll find the job easier indoors. You might like a cup of coffee too."

"Will I be imposing, Sister Claire?"

"Not at all, Sweetheart"

"Thank-you very much, Sister Claire. I'll be most grateful!"

56BIS RUE BONAPARTE

....

"*S*o here we are!" instructed the hostess with fiery-red hair beneath veil, ushering her disheveled-guest inside with sweep of right arm. "Our home isn't exactly *Airandel Castle* in Westmorlandshire, or *Airandel House* in London but Leopoldine and I find it nice enough. Leopoldine's currently off in Quebec where she was assigned to establishing our sisterhood in North America."

The secret-duchess and her buddy the former-nanny rented a fourth floor apartment in an early nineteenth century residential building with black tiled mansard roof situated on Rue Bonaparte—one of the narrow, serpentine passageways of the *Latin Quarter*. The apartment consisted of a front foyer with side closet; a kitchen; a living-room; study; a bedroom; and bathroom. Because of the angle at which the windows were placed, the apartment was throughout spring and summer bathed from an early hour in brilliant sunlight. In late autumn and through winter, it was without the use of lamps, engulfed in darkness almost as soon as sun retreated behind neighboring roofs. One wall contained bookshelves filled with learned tomes, scholarly journals from floor to ceiling.

Pascale adjusted her skirt, put back on heels after climbing four stories.

Acknowledging her friend's hospitality with gesture of gray-green eyes, she then entered.

"Do you like Balzac?" inquired Sister Claire.

"Yes indeed but I'm far from an expert. I just enjoy reading good stories."

"Well, a number of Balzac's novels are situated in this same neighborhood! Most of the streets and a good many of the buildings are still here, too! Sometimes I like to wander about and locate where famous characters lived and fictional events were supposed to occur. Quite exciting! I've gotten to the point I practically expect Pere Goriot, Cousin Bette, Rastignac, Vautrin or Lucien de Rubempré will ask me over for dinner!"

"Awesome!"

Pascale smiled while removing hatpin.

"Out—*that* window" continued Sister Claire, musing, "you see spires poking out above all the centuries-old mansard rooftops. Rising majestically above this cruel, humdrum materialistic world, reaching for the sky! Beautiful! Out—this other window—you can see where in 1968 the students gathered for—*The Days in May*. Literature, architecture, history all-wrapped-up! All a romantic like me needs! That is except for you, of course!"

Pascale acknowledged with lively gray-green eyes. Headgear removed, her immense flowing black locks were certainly in sorry disorder.

"And that do you do at the desk over *there*, Sister Claire?"

"That's where I write my articles," responded friend with hair screaming-red. "Sister Jeanne Navarro appointed me and Leopoldine to direct all our sisterhood's affairs in France, Germany, Belgium, the Netherlands and Luxemburg. This responsibility requires me not only frequently contributing articles to the magazine published by our Order but to write articles appearing in the general press." She halted much embarrassed, before continuing uneasy: "Your 'pious,' 'noble-hearted' Sister Claire has become a regular scandal-mongering journalist. She's become a regular tawdry scribbler. The only thing distinguishing your 'devout' Sister Claire from a traditional *Grub Street* hack is that she wears a crucifix."

"Awesome!" declared Pascale, not at all displeased with the Sisters of the World making a bid to capture a wider, broader, more secular readership.

"They're beginning to mount-up aren't they?" erstwhile-Lady Mary Preston remarked, a trifle embarrassed when pointing to large number of manila folders collecting atop desk, each containing significant number of press statements.

"Indeed!"

"Another's due out Friday."

"Is journalism enjoyable, stimulating, Sister Claire?"

"I must admit, it's, terrific fun seeing your name in-print. Of course it would've never happened without you Sweetheart!"

"And what's the file cabinet for, Sister Claire?"

"It contains among other things the manuscript for a biography I wrote" said author in confessional voice. "It also contains Xerox-copies of the original documents and oral history interviews on which I base my findings. I've lugged that material around with me for quite some time. I guess it's the closest I'll ever come to understanding what it's like being pregnant!"

"The manuscript is important to you?"

Since her protégée brought up subject, the author couldn't resist elaborating. "I'm writing a biography of Sister Jeanne."

"Awesome! It's time one be written! You're in exactly the right position to do it."

"I'm honored, Sweetheart. I tried persuading Sister Jeanne writing it herself but she's too modest about her literary abilities. She gave me permission to tell her story on condition I'm absolutely truthful, don't try glorifying her. 'Write only the truth' she told me. 'I've nothing to hide. If I've done wrong I deserve my faults be shown. Tell how I struggle as hard as any feeble mortal to effectively show Witness to Christ and not purely advance my own selfish ends. I can rely on to tell my flawed-story.' That's a solemn task. But the more solemn a task it is the more I feel I can write the story well and write it justly."

"I'm most impressed" commented Pascale. "You're Sister Jeanne's 'Boswell.'"

"I already put several years into writing it. I've collected a lot of information—personal correspondence, oral histories, diary entries, government papers, interview notes—never previously appearing in any book. If I do say so myself, this, is, the definitive biography of an extremely important individual."

"Awesome! Do people like it?"

"Many noted-professors, theologians, noted-biographers and literary figures in both Europe and the United States say my manuscript is very good! They say I've written an excellent biography of Sister Jeanne. Because of my closeness to her and awareness of the obvious attacks critics might level at me because of that closeness, I was especially careful with my research. Sister Jeanne will be most pleased, most approving. She instructed me to 'tell the meaning of *True Socialism*.'"

"And?"

"Unfortunately, commercial editors claim readers don't like in-depth biographies of contemporary individuals. Considering the *Vocation* Sister Jeanne embraced, I've no juicy sex scandals to describe. University presses insist they can't afford accepting anything longer than two hundred-and-seventy-five pages. That includes: title page, table of contents, footnote pages and index! As for the official Roman Catholic press? Save for Cardinal Blanchard, the hierarchy wants nothing-t-do with *radical* Sister Jeanne. The doddering bishop of Strasbourg even excommunicated her."

"I'm so sorry, Sister Claire. I certainly know what it's like experiencing rejection."

"Of course I might also later write a biography about someone else. And this *someone else* is a uniquely talented young lady. A manuscript recounting her beautiful, inspiring yet so unexpected story will find a lot of eager publishers."

Sister Claire took a large hairbrush from atop walnut chest of drawers with brass drawer handles. She signaled Pascale sit down beside on oak framed couch; next, set about weighty task of untangling the girl's knotted shin-length jet-black hair.

Brush, brush, the nun's brush of girl's hair, brush, brush

Framed, glossy photographs hanging on the opposite wall caught Pascale's attention. One eight-by-ten-inch glossy, displayed Sister Claire's childhood guardian Uncle standing with Franklin Roosevelt, Winston Churchill and Harry Hopkins on the deck of *HMS Prince of Wales*.

Together, the statesmen were signing the *Atlantic Charter*. Another picture, taken in Iran, showed Sister Claire's Persian Auntie dressed as Esther standing amidst the ruins of Persepolis. A third image, captured Sister Genevieve, then still nanny Leopoldine Fauré, pushing a pram in London's *Regent's Park*. Along with these, was an entire series of even larger, framed, glossy color photographs recording Pascale's own various triumphs.

The series might easily be the work of a proud Mama celebrating her child's successes. These images were set apart from the rest, provided an individual domain on the wall. To To the left, above the collection was a crucifix and above to the right, a portrait of the Virgin. Upon noticing Sister Claire curtsey and cross herself each time looking at this veritable shrine, Pascale felt terribly embarrassed.

"Don't worry, Sweetheart" assured the nun hard at work with hairbrush. "Don't feel embarrassed. It's the least you deserve in my home." Girl motioned to object but was silenced with a firm, decisive maternal "hush!"

The veritable shrine included photographs of Pascale/Little Marie on opening night of the public exhibition of the New Arena Chapel. In addition, the reliquary displayed likenesses of her appearing at the public unveiling of her frescoes dedicated to relief of famine and civil war in East Africa. Also contained in the tabernacle, were images of the girl's work bringing attention to spousal abuse, child labor, political injustice. These, and other offenses against individual and communal human rights, the young artist was meticulous viewers understood, were perpetrated not simply in *benighted* far-away lands but also at modernized, *enlightened*-home. Ultimately, like all great art, however, Pascale's offspring provide the world a beauty and spiritual relevance both timeless and timely. She teaches a lesson in her frescoes and engravings sure to be as critical a thousand years hence, as today.

"I could never be successful without help from you and the others, Sister Claire!" insisted *Chere Petite,* once abandoned to own immature, inexperienced-devises in a foreign land. "My success as much belongs to you, Mama, Duchess Charpentier, Mme. Matilda, Sister Genevieve and the others who from the goodness of their heart took me in, freely chose becoming my new family and protectors. You, Mama, Duchess Charpentier and the others deserve as much if not more credit for what I've managed to achieve than me. I'm only your vessel and a *weak* vessel at that."

"Nonsense!" reprimanded Sister Claire. "Don't babble foolishness!" Her voice was as protective, shielding as admonitory, corrective. "We didn't rescue you Sweetheart. You rescued *us*! Any success we achieve is only attained through your blessed intervention."

Brush, brush, brush yet further dedicated brush of girl's massive hair

"I likely shouldn't be telling you this, Dear" revealed the nun, "but Mme. Castellane wants me and Sister Genevieve persuading you to enter our Order."

"I know."

"You do?"

"Yes, from the beginning, Sister Claire."

"So it's no secret what Mme. Castellane desires?"

"No, Sister Claire, it isn't. Please don't tell Mama though."

"I promise."

"Thank-you, Sister Claire."

"You were never angry at any of us, or thought you're being pressured?"

"No, Sister Claire"

"Good, since neither Sister Genevieve nor I believe you have a *Vocation*."

"Neither you nor Sister Genevieve believe I have a *Vocation*?" instantly responded Pascale sourly, much taken aback.

If she currently invisible beneath a thick, shin-length mane of jet-black hair, her abrupt twist of body, angry change of tone in voice indicated hearty-disagreement with friend's assessment. While unenthusiastic about becoming a nun, embarrassed at discovering a veritable-shrine created in her honor, Pascale still felt offended at what she thought was so poor an evaluation of her spiritual, intellectual and emotional strengths. Should Véronique eventually prevail upon her surrogate-daughter to take holy orders, Pascale's—reflective, philosophical character; lifelong devotion to Roman Catholicism; years of selfless service to the Church—made it obvious she was more than capable of fulfilling religious vows. Even her long, bitter conflict with God served making Pascale far more determined seeking Him out as an active, critical element of life than were she an unimaginative, unquestioning *Rosary*-mumbler. Such heterodox personal qualities would be especially helpful too if, joining the political-activist, socially-engaged sisterhood founded by Sister Jeanne Navarro.

"Pardon me! Pardon me!" implored Sister Claire, hastily reorganizing her sentences. "I meant to say neither Leopoldine nor I believe you possess a *traditional* vocation. We both understood this from the first moment we each looked upon your fresco of *The Nativity*. Leopoldine and I knew from that moment that while the artist of this masterpiece was clearly meant to dedicate her life to God, her *Vocation, Calling, Summons* lay in a capacity other than as member of my and Leopoldine's Order."

"So you and Sister Genevieve really *do* think I've a *Vocation*, Sister Claire?" entreated Pascale in humble voice, anger given way to sense of guilt at not being more trusting of her older siblings. "So you think I definitely *am* called to be God's servant?"

"Of course! You've a *Vocation* infinitely higher than my own."

"Please-please-please tell me what it is, Sister Claire! Please-please-please tell me how I'm selected as God's ervant? Tell me and I'll begin this very moment!"

"You've already embarked on your mission."

"I'm already embarked?"

"Yes, my Divine Child. You're mission is to lead *True Socialism*. I came to realize this was all determined long ago. So no more foolishness! From this moment simply trust yourself in the hands of God. Let events flow as they were intended."

Sister Claire set down the hairbrush and walked toward the kitchen. "Let me cook us dinner. You mustn't go home on an empty stomach. A child, even a *divine* one requires nourishment."

LIKE AN EVER-FLOWING STREAM

*P*ascale threw a heartfelt kiss, waved eagerly from inside taxicab window.

Sister Claire threw back an equally-tender kiss, waved maternal from curb.

Precious tears ran familiar sets of feminine gray-green eyes.

Two voices choked.

"I love you!"

"I love you too, *Sweetheart!*"

Taxicab was off.

Sister Claire continued waving until the taxicab delivering her unique friend back to *La Nouvelle Heloise* vanished into soupy darkness, until sound of the car's retreat was heard no more. Then, adopting a serious, pensive facial expression, Sister Claire meditated on the significance of what transpired that afternoon and evening. How long did she remain near frozen in place, consumed in thought? Maybe it was five minutes. Possibly, it was longer.

At last, smiling wide, the pensive British expatriate walked home at normal confident, imposing gait. Left hand soon clinched into fist so it could regularly strike open right palm. It was the same unconscious physical motion she always displayed after reaching a major decision and resolving how best it brought to positive fruition.

"Christ doesn't want us to forsake our world" the nun whispered in *BBC* English, advancing rapidly the narrow, serpentine *Latin Quarter*. "Christ commands his followers to *engage* our world! Christ commands us to *embrace* all its misery! Flight from unpleasant situations—choosing to sit back and allow others solve humanity's moral dilemmas, crises, assuaging our guilty consciences with charity donations or spending hours in self-absorbed, self-gratifying prayer behind the safety of thick convent walls, is not where Christ calls us! No! We must act! What was it that Simone Weil, wrote? Oh yes, 'I *act* therefore I am.'"

"We must each and all of us take assertive action!" declared Sister Claire, melodic voice soft but firm. "Each of us must personally demonstrate our *proclaimed*-love for others. We must all of us personally, demonstrate the sincerity of our *announced*-wish improving the lives of the poor and oppressed. We must act! Otherwise, our faith is just hypocritical babble and fear of death! Otherwise, we're no better than those bigoted, eavesdropping-crones Mme. Rameau who still claim—'I thought it was *resettlement in the East.'* We must each of us struggle for our cause! And ultimately, even if we fail, we only *fail* as the pagan Romans believed the Martyrs *failed.*"

"Yet now that *The Messenger* is arrived" exclaimed Redhead, schoolgirl skip in her step, bounce in long, fiery locks, "I feel to the bottom of my soul we will *not* fail! I genuinely sense we shall *not* fail this time! All which Leopoldine, Sister Jeanne, Mme. Castellane, Duchess Charpentier and the others are pledged to achieve will at last be fulfilled. And fulfilled soon too around the entire planet!"

Unlike the other ladies in the neighborhood carrying in handbag a picture of a child, lover, a good luck charm, or, set of *Rosary* beads—Sister Claire had within her satchel a treasured photo of Pascale. After removing the icon so she might deliver it several fervent, intensely reverent kisses, she confided to the holy image: "Yes my Therese, the victory—*our* victory—*your* victory –is soon to materialize! It won't be long before the entire world is aware of the beauty you create. It won't be long until the whole world honors your message, until all humanity wishes only to hear your call!"

Returned to Rue Bonaparte, Sister Claire sat down at a huge, walnut, antique *secretary*. This intricate, hand-carved, paneled, many-faceted desk, was a gift from Uncle and Auntie. Besides four deep drawers to the sitter's left and right, another extensive drawer was in the *secretary's* middle. At the far end, were additional shelves and drawers for books and magazines, a filing cabinet, a combination safe, and yet more shelves and drawers. Sister Claire only agreed accepting the valuable as well as immensely useful piece of collectable furniture on condition Uncle and Auntie donate it to their niece's religious order. Atop the mammoth writing surface at present were: a pile of important business and political correspondence; a long series of dog-eared scholarly tomes; an anthology of Anna Akhmatova and Marina Tsvetaeva poems printed in Cyrillic, this last item, was a gift from Auntie. Found too, in a separate jumble of written material Sister Claire alone could sort, were: many cut-out, much-underlined articles from French, British and other prominent European newspapers, intellectual magazines, learned quarterlies. Most were authored by Sister Claire herself though she published under the sobriquet: *Magdalene Corday.*

This evening, Sister Claire wrote a letter not to a high government official or director of an influential journal, but instead, to the Superior of her own religious Order.

"*Dear Jeanne*" began the Red Virgin, emotionally-charged sentences fast set down on stationary composed in elegant feminine calligraphy. "*I just received incontrovertible evidence demonstrating the correctness of what has been for me a long deeply cherished hope. It is much prayed for wish. Namely, that my little friend, the painter Marie Castellane, wishes to dedicate all her matchless, unspoiled gifts to the service of our Sisterhood. This splendid child is an inspiration for all humanity!*"

I

"*God grant me grace I fear not the coming battle*'" recited Pascale the words of another Little Flower asthe taxicab navigated soupy blackness.

"Why can't the good ladies be satisfied with me becoming a great artist!" lamented their ward, tears of pain and bitter frustration running pretty teenage face. "I wish Sister Claire, Mama, Mistress and the other good ladies would just allow me to be myself. I know I've been entrusted with a special mission to perform. But I wish the good ladies would allow me to accomplish my mission as I know I was both meant and know I'm most able."

"I'm an artist not an office-seeker!" she wept. "I hate icky politics! I just want to be a painter! But now people want me to be a politician, too! Now people also say I must be a rascal-politician! I wish I could get out of this situation but understand I can't. It's not my decision anymore. My life is no longer my own. It now belongs to others."

"I'm no saint!" cried Pascale. "I'm certainly no saint! Let alone the liberator of the world! But if the ladies who love me, rescued me, protect and nurture me believe I'm a saint, how can I refuse them? They love me. They recognized the full depth and breadth of my talent before I did! I've only come into this position, I've only achieved my fame and distinction, because of those who love me."

"Saint is clearly the role they need me assuming. If all those who protect me, look to me for inspiration, desperately, passionately need believing me their saint and savior, I've no alternative but providing them at least a plausible performance?"

"*'God grant me grace'*" repeated Pascale, *"I fear not the coming battle.'"*

THE PASSION

....

"*F*rom where did you travel to view these marvelous frescoes?" asked a television reporter to someone in the long snaking-line of tourists.

"London"

"And from where did you travel, Monsieur?" TV reporter queried another visitor.

"Athens."

"Kiev" volunteered a third.

Originally arriving from different cities in Europe—Rome, Barcelona, Milan, Lisbon, Madrid, Berlin, Dublin, Copenhagen, Stockholm; soon from—New York, Montreal, Tokyo, Mexico City, New Delhi, Cairo, Buenos Aires, Seoul, Manila, Bangkok and countless smaller towns and villages on separate continents, crowds daily flocked to to see the compelling frescoes by an artist now almost-universally called—*Little Marie*.

Appeal was worldwide. Both her religious works like the New Arena Chapel and her public-commissioned murals gracing central Paris, forever captured a privileged home in the pondering human imagination. Women and men; girls and boys; old and young; *experts* and newcomers to the appreciation of art; rich and poor; each and all discovered a lasting personal attachment to these great paintings. Nor was this passionate attraction restricted to Roman Catholics. Or, to Christians for that matter. Viewers of devout belief as well as none at all, were similarly drawn to these frescoes of exceptional, yearning, thought-provoking beauty.

Equally intense, was the personal affection each viewer acquired for the frescoes' shy, pint-size-artist. She: a bold, uniquely-creative genius with bobbysocks, a revolutionary path-breaker often invisible beneath ocean of tangled hair, as wise as she was deceptively naïve. Most considered Little Marie/Pascale a mystical, ethereal being not just a regular mortal; thought her a noble-hearted, vulnerable and ultimately otherworldly creature; a holy visitor sent from a higher dimension. One, wishing to provide a fallen earth priceless benefit from afar. Such a fragile "Virgin of the Seine" required sheltering love, physical protection, as much as infinite respect, unquestioned loyalty. If it a name Matilda, Véronique, Raymonde, Sister Claire and Sister Genevieve first christened their protégée, soon the General Public too called her the Divine Child. For growing numbers, she was—*my* Divine Child.

Increasing numbers beyond the original "five good ladies" believed this singular girl was humanity's four-foot-ten-inch redeemer. If followers often used different characterizations, alternate metaphors describing *Chere Petite* and her mission on earth, all such varied sentences possessed an identical meaning. Ever-mounting numbers of women and men belonging to the political and intellectual Left, or engaged in civil rights, antipoverty and antiwar movements, in social reform circles, in feminist organizations, many among the unemployed, the homeless, or those who like the diminutive painter herself were rendered refugees—came to regard Pascale as *The Messenger, The Songbird.*

The *Songbird* delivers sweet, charming melodies, not irritating, skin-crawling screeches; she brings news of coming liberation not reason for despair. True saviors also don't discredit themselves by seeking electoral office. Given no choice but performing the mystical role she assigned by ever-growing millions, Pascale never attempted climbing down from her pedestal. Refusing to endorse any parliamentary bloc or electoral candidate, she also declined comment on any national policy or government legislation. Never lending her name to partisan petitions, she also created no art works of blatant partisan advocacy. Pascale seldom appeared in public. On those few occasions she did participate in a march or demonstration, it was just in capacity of ordinary foot soldier, standard able-bodied seaman, dog's-body. Through standing above fray, the artist came to exercise vast indirect power, wide unofficial influence.

Whenever the *Songbird* considered it her grave responsibility issuing a statement to the press, she delivered it in the form of yet another fresco. A masterpiece in paint and plaster, adoring crowds hastily went to view with their own eyes and millions more pondered its deeper philosophical/cultural meaning as the image was reproduced in photographs, postcards, in newspapers, on television and in films. If now largely withdrawn from the world, the artist's voice, physical presence were still daily visible in public murals and on the walls of churches.

Although vehemently insisting "government is for people with trousers," current events relentlessly propelled Pascale to the center of "icky politics."

"Dear Lord" she prayed nightly, "I know we're no longer precisely best-buddies. Dear Lord, I know I've called you a number of bad names, shouted, waved my fist, stuck out my tongue at you. However could you still please somehow find it somewhere in your heart to listen when I once more ask respectfully, humbly—*Grant me grace I fear not the coming battle.*"

I

Obeying first signal from Véronique, Pascale carefully pulled a gray rope.

A large beige canvas fell away from wall revealing newest fresco.

Dignified crowd assembled, clapped hearty-approval.

Photographers from national newspapers frantically snapped cameras.

Newspaper reporters scratched notes.

Obeying next signal received, artist, once more huge red satin bow in ocean of jet-black hair, acknowledged compliments with a demure smile, humble bow of head, deep curtsey.

"Such a perfect, respectful, exquisite young lady my Sweetheart *is*!" observed Véronique, enthusiastic but tender. She beamed all maternal justified-pride, refined feminine joy. Fond genteel tears raced the prima ballerina's unblemished cheeks. "Such a splendid child my Little Marie is! Now nothing can prevent my *Precious* from fulfilling her holy mission."

"*Did I perform well, Mama?*" entreated surrogate-daughter's winning, gray-green eyes. "*Did I perform it as you taught me?*"

"*So you certainly did, Mama's treasure!*" answered parent's wet brown eyes.

After cooking breakfast at her pension and making visitors' beds, the proprietress of *La Nouvelle Heloise* devoted most of the day to honing her ward's artistic gift. From instant first catching her sight, Véronique understood Pascale was—a *lady*. Not one according to the trivialized, much-abused modern definition but—a *lady* in the true, noble, chivalric, courtly love sense. A *lady*—in the form Dante, Petrarca, Shakespeare and Ronsard celebrated in immortal verse.

This afternoon, Véronique rightly savored the victorious emotions sweeping lovely body, genteel soul as adoptive-daughter once more demonstrated herself as perfect a *lady* as any imagined in poetry.

"Bravo! Bravo Mistress's *Robin Redbreast*!" piped La Duchesse enjoyably teary-eyed. She was dressed in immaculate white from broad chapeau to high heels, kid gloves and *Hermes Birkin* handbag to natural pearl earrings and long necklace. "Hurrah! Hurrah! Mistress says: hurrah!" peeress chirped, applauding as vehemently as aristocratic feminine beauties in photographs taken by Gordon Parks for *Vogue* are permitted. "Hurrah!" she told Véronique. "Isn't *Pet* sublime, Firebird-love?"

"Yes, truly sublime, Rose-love!"

The twin spirits nodded to one another in enthusiastic agreement. "Sublime! *Our* Little Marie is, sublime!"

Assembled crowd once more applauded heartily.

"Now wait, wait Sweetheart!" instructed Raymonde, taking a complicated Japanese gadget from *Hermes Birkin* handbag. "Don't move

Robin Redbreast. Mistress wants to take photographs of *Pet* for Sister Madeleine."

Still bending low in graceful deep curtsey, Pascale, wearing a white dress, white bobbysocks and heels, huge red satin bow in hair, complied.

"Excellent, excellent!" proclaimed Raymonde snapping-away an entire roll of film. Once it exhausted, she speedily refilled camera with fresh roll and began snapping again. "Excellent, excellent! I know I've captured some unforgettable images of you priceless creature. Ones preserving you beyond all time and space!"

Sister Claire, today wearing her long veil and habit, motioned for silence.

"Speaking for all those present" announced the British nun in French so faultless it appeared her native language, "I can confidently say Little Marie's gracious decision to donate to our parish garden her latest fresco is a tremendous honor and privilege. I know this work will grace our parish long after we're all dead and forgotten."

As the audience clapped, Véronique in short pink outfit, Raymonde in white one, embraced warmly. The pair rocked gently, softly back-and-forth, the two coalescing into a single graceful feminine body. Besides individual voices and breasts emitting one tender communal purr of joy, Firebird and Olympia each beamed all justified-pride, rightful sense of maternal fulfillment.

Miniature artist nudged reticent Matilda forward, offering former chance airplane seating-mate encouragement with eager teenage gray-green eyes, dedicated adolescent red painted lips.

"Ladies" announced Sister Claire, "a most-esteemed alumna of the University of Heidelberg, distinguished lecturer there and at the Sorbonne, noted historian and our cause's most untiring, vocal and effective champion in the National Chamber of Deputies volunteered making a few remarks. I refer of course to Professor Matilda-Gisela Eisenberg."

At last reluctantly obeying invitation, Brendel's Daughter wearing a light gray professional woman's power-suit, black high heels, stepped forward. "Some of you know me already she began tentatively. If never at loss for words in the lecture hall, on the hustings, during television interviews or in parliamentary debate, appropriate sentences on this important occasion suddenly fled. "I wrote a statement Sisters, Madames, Messieurs" she began again after minute, haltingly. "But in the end decided it best simply speaking from my heart."

Pascale quietly signaled her scholarly friend, approval. As on first occasion pair crossed paths, a comforting, magical aura emerged from the teenager's body, it expanding outward until bringing adult observer entirely within own other-worldly parameter. This was an enchanting light made all the more striking through the fact girl emitting beam was unaware it existed.

"When I first met Little Marie by pure chance on a flight from Frankfurt to Paris" continued Matilda, once more within an aura as brilliant, sheltering as it was to all but a privileged few, unseen, "I never expected being allowed playing a minor role accompanying the remarkable Sweetheart's on her memorable journey. It's been a tremendous experience. People say—'you can't go against the odds'— say: 'talent alone, talent without influence in high places, will get you nowhere.' People claim that when the odds are set against you, the powerful patrons lacking, the money unavailable, there's ultimately 'no way to win, try as you might.'"

"As you all know, I've never been particularly spiritual" she confided. In truth, from the moment of her encounter on the airplane, Matilda privately acknowledged that despite so many angry, vehement denials, she received a clear, personal summons from beyond time and space. One, heard beckoning she embrace its loving bosom since Matilda's earliest memory. "Still, I must admit Little Marie without doubt possesses a Calling, She's without doubt been chosen, selected, anointed by some sort of a greater force, higher dimension to carry out a great, timeless mission. The entire world is going to forever be in her debt. I not only look upon Little Marie as a superb artist, I honor her as the one finally bringing me—"

"Lord!" cried Sister Genevieve, while photographing event for family in Rouen.

"Allahu Akbar!" shouted a scruffy, intruder wearing baseball cap, tattered blue-jeans, old sneakers, raggedy sweatshirt. An angry, zealous look on face same complexion as his target, the intruder forced his way through an unsuspecting, unarmed crowd and before anyone could react, fired a large handgun at his victim's head. Both willing and eager he be recognized for committing the act, the assassin didn't try fleeing. Putting up no resistance as he soon was grabbed by several men, thrown to the stone ground and held prone. "Allahu Akbar! God is great! The Zionist, uncovered she-devil, the satanic bitch-false messiah is no more!"

"Call the police!" screamed one witness. "Call the police!"

"Call an ambulance!" pleaded another. "Quick, call an ambulance!"

"A man shot Little Marie!" was, shout of third witness, in horror.

"Little Marie's been shot!" yelled fourth.

Pascale lay on the stone ground, bullet in right temple. Her legs twitched. Arms trembled, wide-open mouth emitted a gurgling sound, her gray-green eyes, stared into space.

Sister Claire fell on knees to desperate clutch fher atally-wounded protégée. "Please don't die Sweetheart! Please don't leave us, my saint, my darling, my precious, love! Please, my own St. Therese, my own *Little Flower*, don't die!"

"Is my baby still alive?" questioned Véronique, too shocked by terrible event to think of more to say. Tears ran the prima ballerina's cheeks. She felt weak-headed, physically-ill, began collapsing but was held on feet in Raymonde's firm embrace. Once clad in immaculate white or soft pink from chapeau to heels, the Kindly Lady and La Duchesse were now splattered their Beloved One's blood.

Pascale's breathing grew faint, intermittent; four-foot-ten-inch body rigid, gray-green eyes motionless; only gurgling from lips provided any indication she still traveled this world.

"Is our little saint trying to speak?" begged Raymonde, still holding Véronique in warm embrace. "Is our darling Holy One trying to speak?"

"I'll see what I can do" offered Matilda, crouching next to Pascale to better hear what came from dying lips.

"Yes please, please, Professor Eisenberg!" entreated the other disciples.

Matilda sensed again being brought within a mysterious, otherworldly aura. A sublime glow not even approaching death could dim its uniquely compelling shine.

"What's our little saint telling the world?" begged the other disciples.

Matilda watched Pascale mumble a final time before her mouth like rest of small body turned stiff, cold.

"What did our little saint tell us—tell the world, Professor Eisenberg?"

Brendel's Daughter pondered how best to describe for history the meaning of those faint quivers on expiring lips. At last, she concluding just one interpretation was appropriate. "Our little saint tells the world—"

"Yes, yes!" pleaded Véronique, Sister Claire, Raymonde and Sister Genevieve.

"She tells the world—'I die for you. I suffer to redeem broken humanity. I command my devoted followers to now go forth. Spread my message of love, spread my call to fellowship among all nations and peoples.'"

If her brief, troubled life on earth come to an end, the larger, greater story of Pascale Kedari was only just begun.